MW01126087

Kellen's Tempting Mate

Iron Wolves Book 3
By
Elle Boon

© Copyright 2016 Elle Boon

ISBN: **978-1533394071**

Kellen's Tempting Mate

ISBN: **978-1533394071**

Kellen's Tempting Mate, Iron Wolves

Copyright © 2016 Elle Boon

First E-book Publication: May 2016

Cover design by Valerie Tibbs of Tibbs Design

Edited by Janet Rodman Editing

All characters and events in this book are fictitious. Any resemblance to actual persons living or dead is strictly coincidental.

Dedication

To all who were ready to read the big bad alpha's story—I hope y'all are ready for it. Kellen is probably my favorite alpha, and I can honestly say I have created a new character inside this book, that I think y'all will fall in love with just as hard. Thank you for taking a chance on my Iron Wolves and enjoy the ride... these men and women are truly my heart and soul.

There are so many I'd like to thank, starting with Jenna Underwood, who has helped me so much. Thank you for all the crazy calls and wacky conversations. Debbie Ramos of course you are a gem and Janet Rodman for loving Kellen as much as me. You ladies rock! To my Bombshells, y'all are the best group an author can have "mwah".

Of course, I have to thank my family... my hubby who is my rock, my kids, and my writing buddy Kally Kay aka my lab who is always at my side to bounce ideas off of.

Huge shout out to my awesome pimping crew, the *Naughty Girls,* you ladies rock! Last but certainly not least my fans aka you readers who are more friends than anything else. Without you I'd just be that crazy lady with a love of unicorns with pink and purple hair.

Love y'all sooo hard.

Elle Boon

Chapter One

Kellen Styles, alpha of the Iron Wolves, known for his iron control, was ready to rip the heads off of two human men he'd never met. It took monumental effort to make his claws retract. His jaw ached to rip into flesh and bone as he listened to Laikyn speak of the doctors she worked with. The way she so casually spoke of a ménage, when he'd thought she was pure and innocent, waiting for him to claim her, made him see red.

He let her soothe her patient, the young woman who'd been attacked and rescued by Kai Swift, the Navy SEAL, and friend to Rowan Shade. If she thought for one minute, she'd be having one in front of her and another behind her ever again, she was sorely mistaken. Kellen would show her what it was like to be taken by a real man. One who didn't need to share a female with another to give her what she needed. He'd wipe them from her mind and show her exactly what she'd been missing since that night he'd let her go. The night he'd found her in a club she shouldn't have been in. A night that would forever be marked in his mind. A night that clearly hadn't affected her nearly as much as it had him. "Mother fucking bastards." He punched his fist into the wall.

He'd told her they were going to have a conversation, but until he could get his anger under control, he wasn't safe to be around anyone, let alone the one meant to be his mate. Maybe he should fly to Kansas City and eliminate the men she'd been with. Maybe then he'd be able to relax. Kellen stomped back to his office, images of Laikyn with her fiery red hair sandwiched between two unknown men had him growling. Several wolves jumped out of his way as he entered the bar, his deep rumble reverberating around the club loud enough, all in the vicinity dropped to their knees. He ignored them, stomping into his office, and shutting the door with a loud bang.

Kellen glared at the door an hour later as one of his best friends entered, holding a full bottle of his favorite liquor in his hand.

They settled down on the sofas across from one another. Deep into the second bottle, Kellen explained to Bodhi what he'd overheard as Laikyn spoke with Alexa Gordon. The twinkle in the dark eyes should've warned Kellen not to tell the other man. However, Bodhi had the ability to read other people's thoughts, and more than likely already knew.

"What the hell do you mean a threesome?" Bodhi asked, his signature bleach blond hair stood straight up on top.

Kellen glared at the younger wolf, not in the mood to repeat himself. Hearing her talk about the two doctors she was partners with had him seeing red. The tumbler in his hand cracked, the glass cut into his palm, blood mixing with the amber liquid spilling onto the floor.

"Fuckin-A," Kellen swore, shaking out his hand.

"Want me to get the good Doc for you?" Bodhi asked.

A growl escaped before he could call it back. "Go for it. You might wanna kiss your balls goodbye before you do though."

"Bodhi, if I were you, I'd get my ass out to the bar and find something else to do than fuck with the alpha. You are definitely biting off more than you can chew," Rowan Shade said. His dark eyes laughing, walking inside the office without knocking.

"I swear to all you hold dear; I'm going to teach each of you some respect." Kellen stomped into the large bathroom behind him, the one reserved for him and those he allowed. After he rinsed the blood off, the large gash was already healing thanks to his shifter abilities. Being the alpha, his powers were far superior to the others in his pack, making him heal even faster than normal. Wrapping a bandage around the now small wound, he walked back out to find someone had cleaned up the broken glass and replaced the tumbler with a new one. Rowan, he was sure.

"What's on your mind, Shade?" Kellen picked up the drink, downing it in one swallow.

Rowan raised his brows. "Maybe I should come back when you're not in a mood."

"Shut it, Ro. What's up?" Kellen walked around to one of the large, overstuffed couches, taking a seat in the middle and waiting for their newest member to follow. Rowan had been accidentally bitten by a rogue group of werewolves, then turned by Lyric Carmichael, Xan Carmichael's baby sister. Kellen and Xan were more like brothers, and therefore the younger female was like a baby sister to him. Not to mention, she was best friends with his baby sister Syn. She'd broken a rule in not informing him when she'd saved the human, turning him into one of them, but Kellen wasn't a bastard, much. He'd known from the first meeting, that Rowan was going to be an asset to the pack. And he'd been proven correct on more than one occasion, in the few short months since. However, he was still the alpha and wouldn't allow anyone to run roughshod over him.

"I think we need to step up security around here and train the entire pack in self-defense. I also understand you think you can protect everyone, and with your enforcers, me included, we do a damn good job," Rowan held up his hand. "However, our women, and younger generation go outside the club, and many even live outside of the town boundaries, let alone within our protection. What happens if they are attacked there, or in groups? We teach them how to defend themselves without resorting to shifting, and with the help of using their enhanced strength, they have a much better chance at survival." Rowan crossed his arms over his chest.

Kellen hated when others came up with an idea he should've, but he had to agree with Rowan. "That sounds solid. What do you need from me?"

"Damn, that was easy," Rowan laughed.

Shaking his head, Kellen sat his empty glass on the coffee table. "I'm a reasonable man. Give me sound advice, and not a line of bullshit, and you're more than likely gonna get the go ahead. Feed me some cockamamie story, and I'll feed you, my fist. See? I'm all reasonable and shit."

"Yep, very sane and all that." Rowan flashed him a toothy grin before continuing. "I've got the facility out at my place, plus I want to stay close to home with Lyric. I'd like to start sooner, rather than later. You want to handle the signups or whatever the hell you want to call them?"

"This is not a democracy, man. I'm gonna tell the pack it's a new thing they will be doing. You tell me the days, and I'll tell them to be there. Just like that." He snapped his fingers. "Anything else?" Kellen got up to refill his drink, raising it in question before pouring his glass. As Rowan gave a shake, he shrugged and topped off his glass, coming back to settle on the couch.

"Alright, I'll talk with Lyric and work out a few days a week. She and I will work together to get a timeframe that'll maximize what's best for everyone."

Kellen waved his words away. "I don't give two shits what is best for everyone, just what's best for you two. Get it done."

Rowan's deep laugh filled the room. "You might want to talk to Lake before you bust a blood vessel."

Raising his middle finger, Kellen made sure he didn't break another glass. He may heal quickly, but that didn't mean it didn't sting just a little. "Go home. I've got shit to do. Women to fuck."

Their newest member ambled out, his cowboy boots barely making a sound on the concrete floors. Kellen kicked his own booted feet up on the table and leaned his head back on the butter soft leather. Damn, he fucking hated the thoughts swirling around in his head. The only female he wanted was a tall red-haired temptress who didn't seem to want him back. Sure, he could order her to come to him, but that wasn't what he wanted. Kellen wanted her to want him the way he wanted and needed her. A mirthless laugh broke free. "Isn't it ironic? The female I want, is so far out of my reach, she might as well be on another planet."

Laikyn heard the growl in the makeshift clinic. She'd know that sound anywhere. Her body came alive. "Damn it. Why couldn't I want a nice normal man?" She wiped down the rest of the room, preparing it for the next patient who might need it.

"Because then we'd be all bored and shit." Syn Styles walked into the room.

It took Laikyn a moment to catch her breath, when she looked at the petite female standing in the doorway, an ache settled in her heart. Syn Styles and Lyric Carmichael were both five years younger than Laikyn, yet both women were much more intimidating. At five feet nine inches, Laikyn was a good four inches taller than the other female, yet she still had no doubt who would win in a fight, and it wasn't her. Karsyn, or Syn to her friends, tilted her dark head, and with eyes as blue as her brothers, stared at Laikyn, waiting for something that only she knew.

"Can I help you, Karsyn?" Laikyn busied herself with taking the rubber gloves off and tossing them into the garbage.

"Please, call me Syn. How are you, Lake?" Syn walked into the room touching the counter, her hands running over everything as if she was memorizing each thing.

"I'm good. You?" She cleared her throat, hating the show of weakness the croak emitted.

Syn laughed. "I'm not going to hurt you... well, unless you hurt my brother, then all bets are off. I don't think you're going to do that, though. Are you?"

What the hell was this? "I'm not sure what the heck you're talking about. Your brother is the alpha. Nobody could hurt him."

The younger female was across the room in a flash. "You keep telling yourself that, dear. However, you and I both know he is more than that. He's much more than *just* the alpha," Syn spat.

"He's my brother, and I'll kill anyone who hurts him. You got me?"

Laikyn may not be an alpha, but she was nobody's bitch. She drew herself up to her full height, gripped the small hand wrapped in her shirt and squeezed. "Listen here, little girl. Don't come in here and think to threaten me. I'd never hurt anyone, least of all Kellen. You want to see who has bigger teeth, then let's do this, but not in my clinic." Her beast came to the front, making her voice sound deeper.

"Oh, I knew you were worthy," Syn said, wiggling her hand and extricating herself.

She blinked down at Kellen's sister, sure the other female had to be crazy. "Do you need meds or something?"

"Or something, but you can't give it to me. I'm serious about hurting my brother, though. Also, you're gonna need to keep those balls you just showed me. There are gonna be a shit-ton of she-bitches who are gonna think you ain't good enough for him. You'll need to put them in their place.

16

You're also gonna need to put the big bad alpha in his place. Trust me on this. If you need anything, holler at me. I'm on your side... unless you hurt him. Feel me?"

Taking a deep breath, Laikyn nodded. "I think you're jumping the gun here. Your brother doesn't want me. Not for the long run, and I'm not in the market for a part-time lover."

"What about two?"

It took Laikyn a few seconds to understand what she was referring to. Her mouth fell open. "Holy shit. How did you hear about them?"

"So, it's true?" Syn's eyes gleamed.

Lake shook her head. "Syn, how did you hear about that?" She thought back to her conversation with Alexa and was sure the other female hadn't spoken to anyone, then remembered, wolves could hear remarkably well. Damn, she prayed Kellen wasn't foaming at the mouth. Her phone buzzed, saving her from answering. The image of a stethoscope was on the screen.

"Shit," she swore.

"A problem?" Syn looked from her to the phone in her hand.

Not wanting to lie, she shrugged. "I need to head back to Kansas City. My partners and I need to finalize my leaving. I accepted a position here at Mercy General, plus I want to be close to my parents when they're here." Not to mention she missed the pack, and Kellen.

"You want some company along for your trip? I could use a vacation." Sadness clouded her eyes.

Laikyn could really use a little buffer between her and the two men. She didn't understand why they wouldn't accept the fact she wasn't interested in them. Hell, she wasn't into them one on one, let alone two on one. Her fantasies were geared more towards one dominating alpha male, who didn't seem to know she was alive. Maybe if he hadn't saved her all those years ago. A shudder wracked her at the memory, but she pushed it aside. The past was just that. Over and done with. You can't change it. You can't live in it. And you sure as shit can't keep beating yourself up over mistakes. She learned from her mistakes and had grown from them. Okay, she may have run hard and fast, but she'd stopped running and was now ready to face her future. If that included Kellen Styles, then she'd be one happy wolf. However, if it didn't, she'd learn to live without him.

"That would be great. Ever been to Missouri before?"

Syn's smile seemed forced. "Nope. When we leaving?"

She didn't start her residency for another two weeks, but she wanted to get everything she could and get back. "How about tomorrow. I can rent a truck and trailer thing. My apartment came furnished, but I sorta have a lot of stuff."

"No problem. You know we can get that packed and loaded in no time. Heck, we could always ask a couple of the guys to come along." Syn stuffed her hands in her back pockets, looking far too casual.

"No. I'd rather just go and get it taken care of myself. It'll only take a day to pack it up. I'd already started before I came here."

"Alright. No need to rent a truck or trailer. I'll pick you up."

Listening as Syn gave her the time she'd be there, Laikyn felt as if she'd been steamrolled. However, having someone she actually trusted and liked with her on the trip back made her feel marginally better. If only Kellen was as amiable as his sister.

*****

The next day Laikyn heard a loud truck pull up outside the house. She looked outside the window, seeing Syn hop down from the driver's side in a pair of skintight jeans and a tank top. Her eyes widened at the shiny black truck. With its turquoise stripes running down the sides and the two big hearts on the back fenders, it should look odd, but it screamed Syn. From her view she could see the interior matched the same turquoise.

"Alright, I'll be back in a few days." Laikyn kissed her dad's cheek, walked outside, and met Syn on the sidewalk. "Dang girl. This is one big ass truck. You sure you know how to drive it?"

"I'll have you know I learned how to parallel park in a rig this size. You can put your bag in the backseat with mine. I packed light." Syn opened the door to the back.

"You're a lifesaver." Laikyn tossed her small suitcase next to the bright pink one in the back.

"Let's roll, chica. I want to get as close to Kansas City as possible tonight. We could make the trip in like ten hours, if you want to drive straight through?"

Laikyn nodded. "Yeah, let's do it. If you get tired, I'll drive."

Syn turned to her. "Listen. I like you, but nobody drives my baby, but me and Kellen. I might trust Xan, maybe even Rowan. But, and this is a big but, nobody else. Especially someone who probably drives a roller-skate for a car." She put the truck in gear.

"I think I almost feel offended."

"Well, don't be. I don't even let Lyric drive my girl."

"How's that working for you?" Laikyn checked her phone was fully charged.

"Oh, it's working great. She has Rowan's and that girl has her own shiny toys." Laughter laced Syn's voice.

By the time they reached Kansas City, Laikyn realized Syn was crazy, in a completely lovable way. And she wasn't kidding about not letting her drive. Which was fine by her.

"Dang girl, you live in a high-rise in downtown? How did you let your wolf out?" Syn asked, awe making her tone higher pitched as they parked in the underground parking garage. Finding a large enough spot for truck and trailer was easy since most residents had two allotted spots.

Her large studio apartment afforded her enough room to shift and roam inside, but she hadn't been able to get out and stretch in the wilds, not like at home. Laikyn missed doing that but refused to tell Syn or anyone how lonely she'd been.

"Come on. We can order some takeout and crash. I'm exhausted," she said more cheerfully than she felt.

They rode the elevator up in silence, their suitcases in front of them. Laikyn had to swipe her card in order to get on the elevator, the security was one of the main reasons she'd leased the place. As the lift reached her floor, a feeling of something not quite right settled in the pit of her stomach. She put her hand on Syn's arm, motioning her to wait. Both of them stayed inside as the doors opened and used their keen hearing along with their heightened sense of smell, before stepping out. On each level there were only six apartments. Four across from the elevator, and one on each side of the elevator. She had one of the larger ones with a view to die for.

Scents hit her, familiar, yet unwelcome. She pressed her finger to her lips and shook her head. Immediately Syn nodded. How the hell could her partners know she was back and already be at her door, she had no clue, unless it was just lucky timing. However, they shouldn't have access to her floor, unless someone let them up. She'd have to talk to the front desk.

Taking a deep breath, she stepped out with Syn behind her. Finding the hall empty, she looked around, breathing deeply for the cologne they favored, and she hated. The apartment across the hall reeked of them, making her acutely aware of just how close they had to be.

Her door was farther down the hall, which she quickened her pace to get to. Syn didn't seem inclined to do the same, making Laikyn want to rush back and pull her forward. Her hands shook as she unlocked the deadbolt. When she entered, the alarm didn't go off. Laikyn knew she'd set it. Her body, already strung tight, was even more so once she realized the air was heavy with the same cologne. The smell was fresh, not weeks old like it should be.

"Nice place, Doc," Syn said.

Laikyn shut the door, engaging all the locks, and setting the alarm. "They've been in here."

Syn dropped her bag, spinning around to face Laikyn. "What the hell do you mean?"

Looking around the space, she went into her bedroom. "Syn, come here. I mean they've been here while I was gone, and not invited I might add."

Syn pinched her nose. "Girl, did they swim in that cologne or what?" She stared at her. "I'm thinking you haven't had them here lately?"

"Try in like months. I had a party that they were invited to. They've stopped by on a couple occasions, for one excuse or another, but never were invited to stay long." Laikyn checked her drawers, seeing nothing out of place. The stacked boxes still looked the same as when she left.

"Okay, this may sound strange, but do you think they might have bugged your place, or put cameras in?" Syn went over to the bank of windows and opened them up. "This will help air out the stink. What the fuck do they think putting all that shit on is doing for them?" Syn opened the door and stepped outside.

Laikyn gasped. "Syn, do you really think they might have," Laikyn stopped speaking as she stood on her balcony, looking back inside. "Shit, it's totally possible. How would we know? I can't sleep in there thinking they are watching us."

"I'm calling Rowan. He'd know what we should look for. Hell, he'll probably be here in no time to check shit out."

She wanted to tell her no, that they were fine, but truth was, she was worried. Yes, they could handle two human men, but she'd always sensed something was off with her partners. They weren't shifters, but they were more than mere humans, of that, she was sure. "Call him."

"It's going to be fine." Syn pulled her phone out. "Hey Lyric, can I talk to your mate? I think we have an issue here at Laikyn's place in Kansas City."

Laikyn stared out at the night. She could see the Plaza lights and had always thought it was romantic the way they glimmered. Now, she wished she was back in South Dakota beneath the comforting shell of family and friends.

Her ears picked up the deep baritone of Rowan Shade, his tone as commanding as Kellen's. She had no doubt he'd be telling the alpha exactly what was going on in no time. Not that she blamed him since Kellen's baby sister was with her.

"Shit, Syn, maybe you should go. I mean, if you got hurt because of me, Kellen would never forgive me."

Syn held her phone out. "Rowan wants to talk to you."

She looked at the phone like it was a rattlesnake ready to bite her before taking it. "Hi, Rowan. What's up?"

"First of all, don't even start that bullshite about splitting up, or I'll personally beat your ass, then let Kellen know so he can too. Second, you need to get your bags and go to a hotel until we get there. If both you and Syn's creep meter is going off, I'd say you are correct. You two shouldn't have gone off without backup in the first place." Rowan didn't tone down his anger, his deep voice growled out each word as he gave her orders.

"Alright. You have my address, and my number. We'll stay at a hotel until you guys get here." Chewing on her lip, she and Syn stared at each other.

"It'll be okay, but I want to stay on the phone with you until you get to the vehicle, then call once you secure a hotel. Do not speak to anyone. Don't say where you're going out loud until you are on the road. I want you to watch your backs and be conscious of your surroundings. Syn's gonna be driving, so that means you have to be her eyes behind, and all around. Got it? We'll be there within hours."

All of a sudden, she felt like she was in some sort of movie, and she wanted to hit pause and find a new one to watch. She didn't like horror movies, always preferring to watch action and adventure, or comedy.

"I need you to answer me, Lake," Rowan growled.

"Yes. I got it." She knew Syn heard every word as well. They made their way back through her apartment, looking through the peephole, before she punched in the code to the alarm system to turn it off. Once they had their bags in hand they walked out together and toward the elevator. Fear of the men coming out of the apartment, while they waited for the doors to open, ate a hole in the pit of her stomach. Syn squeezed her hand, neither of them breathed as they waited. Just as the door swooshed open, Laikyn heard a lock down the hall disengaging. She and Syn rushed inside, pressing the G button and the button to make the doors shut. The same cologne wafted toward them, letting her know the apartment door across the hall had opened. By the time they reached the ground floor her nerves were frazzled, but she kept the line open with Rowan, his steady breathing kept her grounded.

Syn tossed her bag in the open bed, foregoing the backseat. Laikyn followed suit. Both ladies hopped in, pulling out of the garage without the trailer attached since they'd disengaged it when they'd arrived.

"Duck down, Lake. They won't recognize me if they see a vehicle pulling out."

Laikyn looked at the floorboard, and her five-foot nine inches self, but did her best to curl up in a ball. The tinted windows would hide her, she hoped. "I'm putting you on speaker, Rowan." She placed the phone in between the seats.

With the music playing, Syn sang along to a rock song, acting as if she hadn't a care in the world. Laikyn stayed down until she felt the vehicle pick up speed.

"You can get up. I'm thinking those two hunky men with bodies to die for are your partners?"

"Did you see them?" She looked behind but saw no other vehicles on the interstate at that time of night.

"Girl, I don't know why you didn't like them, other than they drench themselves in cologne, cause damn, they were fine. If that was them. Are they brothers?" Syn asked.

Nodding, Laikyn pulled her hair into a ponytail. "They're supposed to be fraternal twins. Although, I swear they're almost identical. Nobody else says anything about their cologne, but I can't stand it."

"I think it's because they're not your mate, or mates. The fact they were at your neighbor's and had clearly been in your apartment, is also weird as all get out. Do you think they?" she stopped and made an obscene hand motion. "You know, like jacked off with your panties?"

"Holy fuck. Where do you come up with this stuff?" Looking at the gorgeous dark-haired girl, she wondered if she'd had someone do that to her.

"Girl, don't you watch TV? All good psychos do that. So, where we are staying the night?"

She let out a deep breath. "Somewhere safe and secure." She named an upscale hotel.

"What do you think, Rowan? I'd rather you approve and not have to switch." Syn's fingers tapped out a rhythm on the wheel.

After getting the, all clear from Rowan, she kept looking back to make sure they weren't being followed. Syn refused to let valet park the truck. "You realize it's crazy not to let someone who is paid to park vehicles do it, right?"

Syn lifted her bag out of the back and tossed Laikyn's down, then hopped out. "Whatever. Have you seen how some of them asshats drive? No thank you. My baby is safe in my hands."

Chapter Two

Kellen glared at his phone. He was sure he'd misunderstood. "Can you repeat that, and please say it slowly. I think that last bottle of Maker's has dulled my hearing." Kellen stepped outside the club, smiling at one of the dancers as she slid past him in a pair of booty shorts.

"You heard me correctly. Your baby sis and Laikyn are in Kansas City and are pretty sure they're in trouble. I told them you and I would be there by first light. I'm assuming you're ready to roll out now, and Lyric is itching to go with." Rowan's tone didn't sound all too pleased with the last bit.

"If you're not ready in fifteen, I'm leaving without you." He headed back inside looking for his second-in-command. Xan had recently found his mate right under his nose in Breezy. Kellen knew the other male was up to the task of stepping up and taking charge while he was gone.

The two lovebirds were in a corner, doing what they'd felt they missed out on for years. Hell, he was sure if he was a few minutes later, the two of them would be doing a lot more than making out. "Excuse me, Xan. Need a moment of your time."

It took about twenty seconds, which was nineteen too long for Xan to lift his head from Breezy's face. His blue eyes glowed. "What's up, Alpha?"

"I need you to step up in my place, while I take care of a couple wayward shewolves who thought it was a good idea, to run off to middle fucking America alone." By the time he finished, all eyes had turned to the trio in the corner. Kellen turned and growled, making everyone lower their heads. "Damn, I am going to paddle Laikyn O'Neil's ass when I get her home. And don't get me started on Karsyn Styles. That girl needs a damn keeper." He shook his head.

Xan looked behind him. "You taking Bodhi with you?"

The big blond walked up with an empty beer bottle in his hand. "We road tripping?"

"If you can be ready to roll in ten, then you can come. Otherwise, no." Kellen spun on his heel.

Heading into his office, he pulled a duffel filled with a couple changes of clothes out of the closet, grabbed his keys to his XV Urban Assault and walked out without a backward glance. The all-black beast was gassed up and ready at all times. He noticed Rowan's big ass truck wasn't in the lot. Knowing the other male would be pissed if he left without him, Kellen shrugged his shoulders as he disengaged the locks. He tossed the bag in the back, unsurprised to see Bodhi walking out of the apartments in the back with his own gear gripped in his big fist.

The other wolf had been human once, but as a child, he and his parents had been camping when they'd been attacked by a pack of wolves. His parents had been killed, but Bodhi, a mere child, had survived and Kellen's parents had taken him in and raised him as one of their own. Bodhi had always had the ability to hear and read others' thoughts, which set him aside from other kids. It had taken him some time to get over his parents' loss, but when he did, he'd embraced his shifter side like a duck to water. He and Syn always butted heads, yet Kellen trusted her with the other male as much as he trusted Xan. When Bodhi had gone off to find his extended family, it had about killed Syn, and broken his mother's heart, but he'd understood. The years he'd been gone took a toll on his sister and his relationship, but he still loved Bodhi like a brother.

Kellen saw the need in Bodhi's eyes each time Syn was near. Kellen liked watching him squirm as he tried to hide his feelings, and his baby sister ignoring the wolf was icing on the cake most days. Of course, he knew it was only a matter of time before they both gave up fighting fate and did what their wolves wanted.

"You ready, or we waiting on Ro?" Bodhi's unusual green eyes searched the parking lot, his voice urgent.

"Rowan can play catch up. We're outta here," Kellen growled.

His phone buzzed as he prepared to pull onto the street. "You on your way or what?"

A deep laugh came through the sound system. "I'm no dumbass. I'm just down the road. Figured you wouldn't be wanting to wait for me. You got someone with you?"

"Bodhi's coming along for the ride. You got your mate with you?" After getting confirmation that he did indeed, Kellen rolled his eyes. "You should learn to wear the pants, Ro."

"It's so much more fun when he doesn't, Alpha," Lyric teased.

"And on that note, I'm off here. I've got the address in my GPS. Get your ass here or I'm leaving without you. When we get to Kansas City, I'll drop you at the apartment, then I'm going to the hotel. I want to make sure the girls are safe. You scan for any surveillance cameras and all that shit. I figure you're much more up to that task than me."

"Got it. We stopping to eat, or driving straight through?" Rowan asked.

Kellen looked at Bodhi, who shook his head. "You two need to stop, let me know and we'll drive separate. Bodhi and I are driving until we reach the girls."

"Nah, we're good. Lyric packed me some snacks." Rowan's satisfied voice had him looking at Bodhi sideways.

He gripped the steering wheel so hard his knuckles turned white. With monumental effort, one by one, he released his fingers, stretching them out to relax the tension in them. If he kept it up, he'd bend the damn thing, and he'd had the vehicle built to survive the apocalypse.

Hours later, after dropping Rowan and Lyric off at the apartment building, they pulled up to a high-priced hotel. Bodhi laughed at the two valets who jockeyed for the keys to Kellen's rig, while Kellen glared at them both.

"Enough. I won't be here long enough to need it parked. Leave it right where it is, and watch it like it's priceless," Kellen said, leaning close to one of them. "Newsflash, boy, it is totally priceless in your eyes." He was sure the half a million it would cost to replace his rig was more than either of them would make in their lifetime.

The well-dressed young man nodded but didn't ask for his keys again. Kellen handed him a hundred-dollar bill. "Good. We'll be back shortly. There'll be a nice tip for the both of you if I come back to find all is as it should be." Kellen pointed at the XV, hearing the beep he kept walking.

"You realize it's probably against policy to allow a vehicle the size of yours to sit out front, right?" Bodhi's head looked left and right as they entered.

Kellen and he drew stares as they entered, the concierge coming out from behind the desk like they were going to rob the place. With his dark hair messed up from the long drive, his tattoos on both arms, and Bodhi with his bleach blond spiked mohawk, they probably looked more like convicts.

"Excuse me, gentlemen, can I help you?" The man asked in a high-pitched squeak.

Bodhi was busy on his phone, a slight laugh muffled behind his hand.

"We are here to get our sisters." A slight lie, but Kellen was not above them.

"What are their names?"

Knowing what their room number was, Kellen thought of pushing past the ass, but didn't want to have to explain himself to the cops. He had no doubt they already had the nine and one dialed, just waiting to hit the last number. He gave him Karsyn's name and showed his own driver's license. While the man verified the girls were expecting them, Bodhi tucked his phone in his back pocket.

A few minutes later his sister came down the elevator with a wry grin on her face. "Hey big bro, I'm so glad you came." She grabbed his hand, skirting Bodhi.

"Where's Lake?" Kellen tried his damndest to keep his growl to a minimum, failing if the looks on the guests' faces were anything to go by.

Syn pulled him to the opening doors before he could scare the humans. "She's upstairs waiting. I figured it would be safer if I came down, than to have you get all growly alpha on her ass in the lobby."

Bodhi burst out laughing.

"Where is my brotherly hug?" Syn pouted up at him.

He stared down at the pint-sized female whom he loved more than almost anything in the world. "You are gonna be the death of some man." He caught Bodhi's unblinking gaze.

"Ha, he'll be a lucky bastard." Syn punched in the number to their floor. Lucky number seven. Kellen grinned, thinking Laikyn wouldn't be agreeing when she found herself over his lap.

Laikyn was sure of a few things. One, she was in deep shit. Two, Kellen was on his way up to the suite, and three, she was in so far over her head. Her palms were sweating as she looked down at her yoga capri leggings and tank top. She wondered if Kellen liked spandex, then shook her head at the wayward thought.

The hair on her arms raised, a clear indication her alpha was nearby. She went over to the bank of windows, letting the light warm her suddenly chilled flesh. Her ears picked up the sound of the card being swiped through the lock. Keeping her back to the door, pretending a nonchalance she didn't feel, Laikyn prepared for battle.

"Lake, we have company," Syn said.

She turned but having been staring out at the sun made it hard for her to see clearly. Blinking a few times, she opened her eyes to find Kellen only a few inches from her.

"Hi, Kellen. I'm sorry to drag you all the way down here. I thought—" Kellen cut her off with one big finger pressed over her lips.

"Mon Chaton, you will find it best if you don't finish that sentence, unless you want to wind up over my lap in front of my sister and Bodhi. As it is, I'm finding it really fucking hard not to do just that." His deep voice sent a delicious shiver from her head, straight to her toes. Damn her traitorous body.

"For what exactly?" Fake it till you make it. She decided to borrow Syn's motto.

Two brawny arms wrapped around her. "For taking off without telling anyone where you were going. For coming here, knowing you had a couple of jackoffs waiting for you, when you don't belong to them. Shall I go on?"

With each word, the blue of his eyes blazed brighter. His wolf and he were obviously having a hard time staying under control.

"Now, Kellen, I know you are the ruler of all, but I needed to get my stuff. I don't see the problem here. I mean it's not my fault they might be stalkerish." She knew her face was a flaming red, and she cursed her light skin.

"A male tends to get possessive of the female he's sleeping with, even if he's sharing her with his brother." Kellen gritted out between his teeth.

Laikyn's heart stopped. "What the hell are you talking about?"

Kellen gripped her hair in the ponytail she'd pulled it up in, forcing her to stare up into his face. The anger reflecting in his would have scared her, if she didn't know it was because he was jealous. "I know about the three of you."

She tried to shake her head, the slight sting to her scalp kept her still. "There was no three of us." She held up her hand, pressing her palm against his full lips. "No, listen to me. They wanted to, but I was never interested." Laikyn let him see and smell the truth of her words. His body moved closer. The air became thick with tension as he processed her words. She could see his mind was working.

"You never fucked either man?" He tugged on the hair he held.

Laikyn shook her head back and forth as much as his hold would allow and licked her lips. "Never."

"Bodhi, take Syn down to the coffee shop in the lobby." He turned his head, not releasing Laikyn as he spoke. "Don't let her out of your sight and stay inside. I need a few minutes alone with Lake."

She was sure Bodhi muttered something about needing more than a few, but her attention was centered on the male before her. His hard body pressed against hers, made it impossible to miss the fact he was fully aroused and knew he could smell her need.

The soft sound of the door closing signaled a green light to Kellen, his head bending, taking her lips in a soul-destroying kiss. She remembered the way his lips felt on hers from years ago. Her mouth opened for his tongue, loving his taste, the expert way he took over.

"You make all my good intentions fly out the damn window, Mon Chaton." He nipped at her bottom lip.

Hearing him say kitten in his deep possessive drawl made her feel special. Over the years she'd made it a game to watch and listen to the women he'd bedded, and none had ever said he called them his anything. Babe, baby, doll, things that he would call any female, but never anything possessive. Not like what he'd called her as he'd taken her virginity, and her heart. She gripped him tighter, rubbing against the large bulge behind his zipper. She knew she should push him away, tell him to go fuck himself. Laikyn had tried to erase the memory of his dismissal all those years ago. However, she couldn't forget what it had been like to belong to Kellen, even for one night. Now, standing in his embrace, she'd gladly do it again if only for just one more day. Her pride be damned.

One of his hands found its way between their bodies, massaging first one breast then the next. She arched into the caress, needing more. Kellen chuckled against her lips. His mouth moving down her neck, fingers splaying on her back with one hand while the other gripped the hardened nipple and pinched. Hard. She cried out, holding onto his shoulders, bolts of pleasure zipped straight to the heart in a shocking wave.

"So responsive. You were the best lover I've ever had. I dream of you," Kellen whispered against her throat, his teeth scraped against the tendon.

Laikyn wanted to feel his teeth sink into her there. "You're all I dream about. Nobody ever measures up to you," she admitted.

The fingers holding her nipple contracted, the pleasure bordered on pain and then he switched to the other, repeating the motion. Laikyn thought she'd come from just that, until he whipped the tank top off, leaving her in a satin bra.

His fingers unclasped the front closure, cool air hitting overheated flesh. She tried to remove his T-shirt, but he bent his head, covering the nipple he'd pinched first and sucked it into his mouth. Her knees threatened to buckle, the only thing keeping her up was his arm behind her back.

"Oh god, Kellen. I think I could come from just that." Her fingers splayed into his dark hair.

Straight white teeth bit down, tugging on the flesh. He growled before doing the same action to the other side. Laikyn felt her body spiraling close to orgasm.

She reached her hand out to rub him, wanting to feel his warm flesh beneath her fingers. The electric shock of feeling his smooth skin sent her over the final step into bliss. She cried out, shocking both of them as her body twitched, needing to be filled.

Kellen worked his hand under the elastic of her yoga pants. The moisture surely coating his fingers, but Laikyn was so far gone she gave no fucks.

"You came." He made it a statement. Awe lacing his voice.

Two fingers slipped inside her. "Yes. God, I want you. It's been too long."

Her hands reached for his belt buckle, asking for permission. His nod had her opening the fastening. The ringing of Kellen's phone made them freeze. With his hand in her pants, hers reaching for the big cock ready to spring free, they stared at each other.

"The only people who'd be calling me would be Rowan, or Xan." He pressed his forehead to hers.

"You should probably get it then." Her voice shook. Her pussy tightened around the digits still embedded inside her.

Kellen slowly withdrew, keeping his eyes locked on Laikyn, he brought his fingers to his mouth and sucked, licking them clean. "You taste better than anything I've ever had." His eyes held hers. "Mine, Laikyn. All fucking mine." Reaching into his back pocket he pulled out his cell. "This better be fucking good."

Rowan stared around the apartment, using the device specially made to detect if there were any listening or video recorders, pleased to find none. His mate followed him around, her cute little ass staying as silent as him, and trying to copy all his moves. If he didn't watch it, she'd be a better soldier than he'd been.

"So, no creepers set up cameras to watch her while she slept?" Lyric asked once they were in the kitchen.

He shook his head. "Nope, unless they came in and removed them after the girls left last night, which is a possibility."

Lyric's shocked expression showed she hadn't thought of that option. "Shit. Is there any way we can find out if there was any in here?"

Hating to disappoint her, he tapped her nose. "Sorry, darlin."

She sighed. "Alright, then we need to do some recon."

Damn, he fell a little more in love with his mate every day. "Do you smell anything off?"

"It reeks of male cologne, which I happen to know Laikyn would not be entertaining any man, who bathed in something this strong." She waved her hand in front of her face. He was still getting used to the enhanced sense of smell and agreed with her. Whoever, or possibly more than one person had been in Laikyn's home recently wearing way too much of the stuff, for even a human.

Rowan froze as he heard the almost imperceptible sound of two sets of feet outside the door. He checked his weapon and looked to see that Lyric had also pulled her own, shiny, specially designed, Ruger from the back of her jeans. He motioned with his head for her to go into the back room as he recognized the smell wafting in. Whoever had been inside while Laikyn had been gone, was back. He planned to show them the error of their ways real quick like and be back home in time to bed his mate.

Leaning casually against the sofa, his gun pointing straight at the door, Rowan watched the big men enter. The shock on their faces was quickly replaced by anger.

"Who the hell are you, and what did you do with Laikyn?"

"I think I'll be asking the questions, pup. Why the hell are you entering someone's apartment without an invitation, and just who the fuck are you?" He let his voice go deeper, the command evident, noticing both men's eyes had an eerie red tinge flash in them for a moment.

"We ain't pups, boy." One of the blond men stepped further into the space.

Rowan stood straight, letting them see he wasn't intimidated by facing two men. "You are in my friend's apartment. Uninvited, I might add. You've been here in the last week, although she hasn't been. Again, uninvited. Now, tell me why I shouldn't call the cops on your asses?"

He watched the two men staring at one another as if they were having an internal conversation, and then it hit him. They were. These two men were not human. Or no more than he was. He sucked in a deep breath, sifting through the heavy cologne to the men beneath, detecting a faint whiff of wolf. However, he didn't think they were a hundred percent shifter. "What the hell are you?" Not one to beat around the bush, he asked the question that needed to be answered.

"My name is Damien, and this is my twin brother Lucas. We are Laikyn's partners at our clinic. She's a junior partner. We came by to check on her." His cultured voice came out smooth.

Lifting his chin, Rowan smiled. "Nice to meet you. Now, how about you answer my question before I get trigger happy."

"Clearly you know we are shifters like you." Lucas spoke up, both men took a step away from each other.

Having been in the military for too many years, not to mention an expert in hand-to-hand, he knew they were going to try to split up and attack him. Rowan sighed. "Ah, boys, I really wish you weren't gonna play it that way." Faster than either of the twins could comprehend, Rowan got off two rounds, taking out one knee on each male as he flipped over the back of the couch, landing on his feet. He pulled out his second gun, each with a silencer attached.

"Now, I know you both will heal quickly, but I can, and will, shoot you both in the heart, and when

I get to the fifth bullet in each one, it's silver. Pretty sure that one's gonna hurt like a motherfucker. Care to try me? We're at number two. Should I keep going, or y'all gonna stop being jackasses, and start talking?"

The one named Damien growled, the sound rivaling Kellen, yet he didn't move any closer. Blood-soaked Laikyn's floor from the wounds, then faster than he'd imagined, they stopped.

"Well played, wolfman." Lucas looked down at his slacks. "These were one of my favorite pairs, not to mention expensive. Who should I send the bill to?"

"I'll show you mine if you show me yours," Rowan said.

Again, the two clearly spoke to each other before looking directly at Rowan. The only difference in them was one had a visible tattoo peeking out of the collar of his shirt. Lucas must be the bad boy of the duo.

"We are what you'd call a hybrid. You're a wolf, newly made from what we can tell. Yes?" Damien asked.

"That's correct. It's been a few months. What else are you? Ahhhh, don't even think about it." Rowan nailed Lucas in the uninjured kneecap. Hearing his yelp of pain didn't faze him.

"Why should we tell you our secrets, when we don't know shit about you?" A tick was throbbing furiously in Damien's cheek.

"I'm down to three bullets in this gun aimed at baby bro here, and four in this one. You both may be fast, but I'm faster, and I'm getting real damn tired of jawing right about now." He could hold the weapons in his hands for hours and not tire, but these men didn't need to know that.

Lucas stood straight. The blue eyes definitely had a strange red hue.

"Easy, Luke. I think we should explain our predicament to the good man, and then go from there." Undercurrents flowed, yet they bounced off of Rowan. He had a strange feeling they were trying to control his mind, which made him grin.

"I'm gonna count to three, then I unload. Oh, and just as a warning, the next bullet out I'll hit the groin, 'cause I fight dirty like that. Not, 'cause I dislike men, but there's a main artery real close. You ready?"

Damien and Lucas placed both hands over their dicks.

"Fine. May we sit down?" Damien gestured toward the kitchen table.

Rowan inclined his head, figuring Laikyn wouldn't mind since the leather and wood was a lot easier to clean than the carpet in the living room.

"We were born, not made. Our mother is a shifter, while our father is... vampire. Yes, I can see you were unaware of our kind, or should I say, our father's kind. Most vampires have found it quite easy to blend in today's society, even with their limitations with the sun. However, our father found his Hearts Love in our mother, a shifter. Vampires and shifters are similar in that regard. We have searched for hundreds of years for our Hearts Love, yet until we saw Laikyn, no one female did it for us. It is prophesized that we will meet one who will complete our trinity. Until then, we will not feel whole." Damien and Lucas rubbed their chests.

He understood what it felt like to want something, and think you'd never have it, but hundreds of years? Rowan couldn't wrap his mind around the magnitude of their situation.

"Alright, let me get this straight. You think Laikyn is your, Heart whatever? Cause let me just forewarn you, my alpha believes she is his mate. Trust and believe he will not let her go without a fight."

Lucas was up and out of his chair in a flash, throwing Rowan against the wall with surprising strength. "If she agrees to test our compatibility, your alpha will have no say."

"Release my mate, or I will shoot your brother right between the fucking eyes, and my gun is only filled with silver." Lyric's voice had gone low.

Rowan didn't release his hold on the two guns in his hands, his wolf pushed to the front. "Release me, or my woman will do just as she said. You may take a bite out of me, but I can guarandamntee you, I will fuck you up two seconds later."

The man's nails lengthened, his eyes were blood red. One by one he relaxed his fingers from around Rowan's throat, then stepped back. "You will allow her to make a choice, or the battle that will ensue will be great. Far greater than any you have faced."

"I'm a SEAL. You don't know what I've faced." He rolled his neck, easing the constriction around his throat. Damn! The bastard nearly crushed his windpipe.

"Rowan, do I shoot this one, or what?" Lyric asked. She sounded as if she was asking for more sugar.

"Come to me, darlin."

"I've never met two with mental blocks quite so strong," Damien remarked.

"And I've never met two men I wanted to shoot quite so bad, it was taking all my focus not to do it." Lyric walked backward toward Rowan.

"Now, I'm going to call my alpha, and invite him to this little party. I think this is going to be a nice little sit down, now that we have more information."

"Luke, come and sit down. I'm pretty sure you and I don't want to be filled with silver anytime soon. Mother and father would be most displeased. We will speak to their alpha and hear what Laikyn has to say."

The blond doc crossed his completely healed legs over one another. "What makes you think she'd choose you now? I mean, she clearly hasn't in all the time she's been here with you, so why the hell would she now?"

With his mate's back to his chest, Rowan felt his wolf settle.

"We were giving her room, and time. Someone thought it a good idea to do this." Lucas shot his brother a glare.

He pulled his phone out and dialed Kellen's number. From the sound of the other man's voice, he was pretty sure he'd interrupted something intimate. Which was a good thing with the way both hybrid men were acting. He hoped like hell Kellen and Laikyn smelled of each other.

The fact they hadn't answered why they'd been in her apartment while she'd been away still needed to be answered. Kellen would take over when he got there, and Rowan knew for a fact the alpha wouldn't allow anyone to take away what he thought of as his.

"You realize my best friend is with Kellen, along with Bodhi, right?" Lyric whispered, even though the others could hear.

Rowan nodded, not understanding where she was going with her train of thought.

Her pointy elbow nailed him in the gut. "I love Syn, but she is more protective of those she loves than I am of my Harley, Pixie. Kellen is at the top of the list of people she loves with me right below him. I think she may have had a talk with you a time or two. Imagine the two of them coming in here, and then imagine Bodhi thinking Syn was being disrespected."

He really needed to make a chart when it came to her thought process. Understanding where she was going with Syn and Kellen, but Bodhi through him for a loop.

"Bodhi has loved Syn since the day he came to the pack as a new wolf. Syn thinks he's too good for her, so she ignores it. One day, he'll catch her, but he will still protect her with his life. Those two across from us." Lyric stared at the twins, deep in their own conversation. "They will be considered a threat. You may think Kellen is going to be the meanest one to enter, but believe me, if Bodhi thinks Syn is in danger, he's the one you want to watch out for."

"Duly noted, darlin." He kissed the side of her neck, inhaling the sweet strawberry scent.

Chapter Three

Kellen loved the dazed look in Laikyn's green eyes. He especially wanted to see her laying on his bed, devoid of all clothes while he pleasured her to distraction. The untimely call from Rowan made him want to throw his phone away. Yet, the other male told him he had the doctors at Laikyn's apartment, and then sent him the information he'd gotten from them.

Son of a bitch. Vampires? Kellen wasn't sure what to think about that situation or the men. Had no idea what their abilities were, but knew he wasn't about to take his mate where the other men were.

"I want you and Syn to stay here with Bodhi." He stopped as Laikyn shook her head vigorously.

"Not gonna happen unless you plan to chain me to the bed." Fire lit her eyes.

Damn, he fantasized about doing just that. "Female, be reasonable." He stepped back before he was lured back to her gorgeous body. The fact he didn't need to bend in half to claim that sassy mouth had him wanting to do it over and over again. Her womanly curves fit perfectly to his harder frame. They were made for one another. If only she'd listen to him, it would be exactly as he'd envisioned it.

She smiled as if she'd read his mind. "I can be really bendable when I wanna be." Her tiny pink tongue came out, wetting her plump lips.

His dick jerked through the opening of his jeans, where she'd worked her hand inside, before the call interrupted them. His tempting little mate looked down, gave a husky chuckle that had his eyes crossing, then trailed her hand over him, cupping his balls. "Did I mention that I promise to not make you sorry, and to listen to you?"

His body responded to her words, even though his brain was screaming at him to say no. The sight of her perfect porcelain skin against his rough denim was an erotic sight to behold. "Fine," he growled.

Laikyn gave him a none too gentle squeeze, remembering he liked it rough. "I'll be a good girl."

"Get dressed and let's go before I change my mind." She bent, slipping the silk bra back on before the tight tank top, acting as if she was ready. He stared at the gorgeous thing in front of him in a pair of tight black leggings that reached her calves, and a spandex tank top that molded to her breasts, showing off every luscious curve. He unbuttoned his flannel top, leaving him in a black undershirt. "Put this on. I don't want those asshats to see what's mine."

A blush stole up her neck into her cheeks, but she shrugged into his top. "Kellen, we are going to have to talk about," Laikyn stopped as he covered her lips with his.

"Later. Right now, we deal with the threat against you, then you and I'll talk. At home." His home, which would be theirs if he had anything to say about it. Jeezus, she looked adorable in his shirt, the thing hung down to mid-thigh, covering her ass. Her hands shook as they worked the buttons into the holes.

"Let me grab my purse." The strap was placed over her neck and across her chest, then she waited for him.

Yeah, she was it for him. He'd wipe out an entire pack of vamp-shifters if they thought to take his mate from him.

Syn and Bodhi stared at them when they entered the lobby, tension in every line of his sister's frame. He pulled her next to him. "What's wrong?"

"Nothing. Where we going?" Syn looked over at Laikyn.

He decided to let it go as Bodhi cleaned up what appeared to be breakfast. "Have you eaten, Lake?"

Laikyn's stomach growled. "We were going to call down for room service."

"Do you like drive thru food?" He wasn't a huge fan, but it would do in a pinch.

They agreed on a chain that was around the corner, then they were on the road to her apartment. The closer they were to the high-rise where she lived, the more he could smell her fear. His XV had bucket seats, making him wish he could pull her into his lap and reassure her all was fine. He opened the alpha link, the one all his pack was on and focused on Laikyn. *"Nobody will hurt you, Mon Chaton. I promise you this. If you sense anything, or need to speak to me, find me here. Only you and I can hear each other."*

She tucked a stray strand of hair behind her ear, several silky lengths had come free from the hair tie from when he'd tugged, because he couldn't resist.

He listened as she instructed where to park, finding his sister's trailer in the spot they'd left it. He glared at the evidence they'd left without proper protection and then at the two women in his rig. Laikyn's hand rubbed his thigh. *"Soothing the savage beast?"*

"Something like that." She smiled at him.

"Hello, it's rude to use your inside voices in the company of others," Syn groused.

Bodhi didn't say a word, his fingers tapping on his phone kept him occupied throughout the ride.

"If you are going to be engrossed with whoever is on the other end, you might wanna stay in the rig, Bo." Syn said with false sweetness, hopping out before Kellen had shut it off.

He met Bodhi's stare, seeing the boiling beneath the green orbs. "I'm gonna spank her ass one of these days."

The door to his XV jerked open, leaving him and Laikyn inside. "That's gonna be fun to watch." Laikyn pointed out the window.

Kellen didn't agree. His hand pulled her across the console, fusing their mouths. "Don't get any ideas from that one, or you'll find your own delectable behind red more often, than not."

"Promises, promises," she said breathlessly.

He maneuvered them out of the vehicle and into the lift, somewhat mollified with the security measures they had to go through in order to get into the building. Of course, there were clearly ways to get in, proven by the twin hybrids up in her apartment.

"Let me lay down some ground rules for you two. I want you both to stay behind Bodhi and me at all times. If something happens to both of us, I want you to take my gun and shoot for the heart. Syn, you know how to shoot, yes?"

His baby sister showed him she had her own gun, looking comfortable with the girlie painted piece in her hand. He nodded. "How about you, Mon Chaton. Can you shoot?"

Laikyn swallowed. "Killing is abhorrent to me, but I can and will. I've been shooting since I was a little girl." She pulled a small silver piece out of her crossbody.

"That's my girl." Kellen tried to restrain himself, but the sight of her holding a gun like she meant business turned him on. Not that he'd actually stopped being hard since he'd been in her vicinity. He watched her put the piece back into the bag, then wrapped his arms around her. Kellen wanted to show her he could be gentle, licking at her lips like the finest wine. She stroked his tongue with her own, making him growl. Kellen lifted her against him, feeling her legs wrap around his waist. He pressed her to the side of the elevator, forgetting the others were inside with them. Kellen was two seconds from ripping the pants off of Laikyn and fucking her right then and there. Luckily, the ding signaled they'd reached her floor. Bodhi coughed, while Syn laughed outright.

"We need to finish what we started soon, dammit." He nipped her lip, a little of her blood entered his mouth.

Laikyn did the same to him, the action making him groan, yet he let her slide down his body. "Be good and remember what I told you."

She saluted him, making him smile. "Save that for Rowan. You can just call me Sir. Yes, Sir will sound lovely coming from your lips." Kellen took her hand in his and let her lead the way with a huge grin on her face.

Laikyn almost forgot where they were while she was wrapped up in Kellen's huge arms. The male was a complete menace to society, yet she was more than willing to let him take charge.

The overwhelming cologne wasn't as strong, like they hadn't sprayed it lately.

"What the hell is that smell?" Bodhi asked, nose in the air.

She rolled her eyes. "That would be my unwanted visitors," she said loudly outside her door.

Bodhi cracked his neck. "Well, it's god damn offensive to my nose."

All four laughed but stopped when they entered. Seated at the kitchen table were none other than Damien and Lucas Cordell. Blood stained one of Damien's knees, while Lucas's right and left were bloodied. Rowan and Lyric stood near the large window seat, guns out and pointed at the two doctors. Lake scooted behind Kellen, letting his large frame hide her, his heat infusing her with much needed warmth.

"Laikyn, we mean you no harm." Damien stood, the chair making a scraping sound on the wooden floor.

"Why are you here?" Laikyn's voice came out in a whisper.

"Please come out and listen to us. You will find we would never hurt a hair on your glorious head," Damien said.

Kellen growled, making the pictures in the room rattle. "She is mine."

Lucas lifted his head and inhaled. "I don't smell a full mating."

"Don't make me shoot you again, dumbass. You and your brother know she belongs to him. Has she ever touched you the way she is touching him?" Rowan asked, waving his free hand toward her and Kellen.

"She never gave us a chance." Damien stared at Kellen, a plea in his gaze.

Laikyn stepped around Kellen. "I'm sorry, Damien, but I don't feel that way about either of you. And let's be honest. You don't really feel that way about me." She softened her tone, seeing they really were nice guys, albeit something was going on.

Lucas sat down with a heavy sigh. "I told you she wasn't the one."

Damien followed suit and sat down at the table as well. "Please sit. You were the first female who we both felt a spark for. I was certain if we spent time in each other's company, it would grow into a Hearts Love like our parents," he said, sorrow echoed in his words.

She almost felt sorry for them but remembered the fear she'd felt last night when she and Syn had come home. "Why were you here last night and how did you get into my apartment?"

"Let's sit down, Mon Chaton. I think this is going to take a while, and I don't feel like standing." Kellen guided her into the living room, taking a seat in the large recliner, pulling her onto his lap.

Assured they were no longer bleeding, the two hybrids got up from the table and joined them, seating themselves on the loveseat across from Kellen, two sets of blond brows raised at her alpha's show of possession. Laikyn squirmed on his thigh until she felt the hard ridge of his erection jump under her ass, and quickly turned to face him. Kellen's wicked grin had her blushing to the tips of her hair. She tried to sit like a lady. A feat that was impossible while draped across two hundred and twenty pounds of pure alpha male bent on showing everyone he was in control.

"Continue with your story, Cordell." Kellen spoke while inserting one hand between her thighs. His scent was driving her to distraction.

Damien cleared his throat. "We'd been informed that a vamp from another enclave was in town. As this is our territory, we were shocked to find this being not only living in the same location as Laikyn, but on the same floor. Most vampires, unless they are hybrids like Lucas and I, cannot go out in the sun. There is a prophecy, which neither my brother nor I buy into, that says twin daywalkers will rule all vampires when they find their Hearts Love. The one being who will complete the trinity. Although Lucas and I have always had a special connection, especially when it came to women, we do not wish to rule the entire population of vamps. Too much work, and neither of us want that type of distraction in our lives. No matter what any of you think, we enjoy being doctors. Well, in this lifetime." He flashed pearly whites with two canines much longer than a normal human.

Syn stepped forward. "What made Laikyn here so special to you?"

Lucas tapped his nose. "She smelled like a shifter but wasn't part of a pack. She's a doctor and is extremely gorgeous. Her body would fit perfectly between the two of us. When we both scented her, our wolves stood up and took notice. That was a first, even though our vamp halves weren't completely on board. We assumed it was because we hadn't shared sex or blood with her, yet."

Laikyn felt Kellen's muscles tightening with each word until the very end. She wondered if he still thought she'd had a relationship with the good doctors.

"I did not think you had anything with them but hearing them describe your attributes makes me want to rip their fucking eyes out." His fingers inched up higher between her thighs.

She crossed her legs to stop his movements. *"Behave."*

"You have years to make up for, Mon Chaton. Behaving is far from what I have planned."

"Are you two done?" Syn sat on the arm of the sofa, Bodhi glaring for all he was worth.

Rowan and Lyric still stood, only now his gun was holstered, while Lyric's was pointed at the floor. "Now that you know she is not yours, explain about this vamp. Do we have a problem?" The ex-Navy SEAL asked the question they all needed to know.

"He is not your concern. We went to his apartment last night, but he was not in residence. His home was set up to withstand the sun. I don't know how or when he'd had steel covering installed, but from what we saw they are timed to come down at the first hint of light. I'm sure he also has it to where they go up when the sun sets." Damien pointed out the windows. "I didn't see a sleeping space but that doesn't mean he doesn't spend his days there, just that he wasn't there when we were there. Vamps don't sleep in coffins, but they do need dark, lightless areas, unlike Luke and me. Our parents were the exception because of their sharing of blood. Which is why shifters don't share freely with vamps."

Tension became so thick; Lake wasn't sure what was going to happen next.

Lucas laughing wasn't the wisest, but he also wasn't the smartest of the twins. "You were unaware of others, weren't you?"

Kellen shifted beneath her. "I keep my pack safe, and we don't fuck with *others* as you put it. If a threat comes to my territory, it is dealt with. Period. I'm assuming they never came through, or if they had, they watched their Ps and Qs."

Confidence rolled off of Kellen.

Damien leaned forward. "I admire your courage, Alpha, but don't be so cocky. Yes, you are strong and could rip off the head of any human, and most shifters. I'd dare say even most vamps, but there are master vampires, ones who are very old and skilled that even Luke and I combined would have a hard time defeating."

In a move too swift and fast for Laikyn to counteract, Kellen was up and had her next to Rowan in seconds. "You think because you are fast you are better than a shifter? You think because you have the power of mind control, it makes you better than me? Try me?" He pulled Damien to his feet.

Laikyn felt a wave of power sweep through her condo, the air literally sucking out of her lungs, making it hard for her to breathe. A trickle of blood seeped out of her nose as she watched Kellen face off against Damien, while Lucas tried to stand, but an unseen force kept him seated. She held onto Rowan and Lyric, her lungs feeling as if they were about to burst. Through the link Kellen had told her to call him on, she thought of reaching out, but worried it would cause him to lose the battle of wills. More blood flowed from her nose, falling onto the flannel shirt.

Kellen's head jerked toward her, his blue eyes a bright electric blue. With one big fist, he shoved Damien across the room. Instantly, she could get air into her starved body.

"Damn it. Why didn't you reach out to me," Kellen murmured, coming to her side, and cradling her to him.

Shaking, she looked around for something to wipe the mess off her face before answering. "I didn't want to distract you."

He carried her to the back of her apartment, knowing exactly where the master bedroom was, and shut them inside without looking back at the people in her living area. "Next time you don't suffer. If you are hurting, you tell me, or," he stopped and sat her on the large counter in the bathroom. "There better not be a next time."

"Yes, Sir, Alpha Sir." She looked at the pale female staring back at her, and the male frantically running water, and barely kept from laughing at the picture they made.

"You are a bad subbie. It's going to take some training, but I think I'm up for the job." Gently, he wiped her face, then neck, making sure he cleansed all the evidence of her blood.

Damien stared at the closed bedroom door and felt a small pang of regret. Not a lot, but a smidgen. "Well, that was interesting," he said, dusting his hands off.

"You are a strange one. You know that, right?" Rowan asked.

He tilted his head to the side. "I have been told that a time or two in my very long life."

The tiny little dark-haired female stood up. He and his brother both inhaled, but their wolves didn't do anything except yawn.

"How old are you exactly?" Syn asked.

Lucas uncrossed his legs, the bullet wounds completely healed. "If we told you, we'd have to kill you." He laughed as the little female with the one named Rowan raised her weapon. Damien was sure her aim was true.

"Luke, I truly do love you and would hate to have to explain to mother what happened to her second favorite son. Imagine the heartache it would cause." Damien injected just enough boredom to piss his brother off.

"Mother only has two sons, asswipe." Lucas stood, ignoring the guns aimed at his head and chest. His brother really was a loon.

"Exactly. Hence why you are her second favorite. I have no doubt if we had another brother, you'd probably be her third."

Lucas flashed across the room, making the two women gasp. Damien was pretty sure the only one in the apartment with the ability to defeat him and his brother was the alpha, but he wasn't willing to test his theory. Besides, he found, much to his surprise, he actually liked the Iron Wolves. They needed to learn about others in order to be safe. Damn, he didn't want the responsibility.

"Mother loves me more, brother." Lucas flicked him in the ear.

Moving with the speed of their vampire lineage, he was behind Luke and had his brother in a headlock. "Dream on, baby bro, dream on. Besides we both come second best to Alecia, the princess, or as dad likes to call her, babygirl."

"Lord save me from stupid men," Syn said. "So, what's the plan?"

Stepping away from his brother, he faced the remaining wolves in the room. "We have rounds at the hospital. I suggest you get Laikyn and her stuff out of here before nightfall. We will handle her paperwork at the clinic and make sure it's smoothed over with the hospital as well."

"Must be nice having the freaky mind control." The little spitfire he wished had sparked their interest said.

"I will admit, it comes in handy."

"Sorry about shooting you and shit," Rowan said, his southern drawl slightly evident.

Damien shrugged. "This is nothing. Try being staked. Once in the early eighteen hundreds I was... never mind. That is not a story for polite company." He winked at the two women then strolled to the door. As he and Luke reached the entryway, he looked over his shoulder. "Ignorance because you are unaware is one thing, but now that you know there is more out there, you need to school yourselves. Yes, you have all been lucky, however, luck is a fickle bitch sometimes."

With those parting words, he and Luke left Laikyn's apartment. Through their twin bond he could tell his brother also wished she was their one, and had they been given the opportunity to have sampled her, he knew she wouldn't have been it. Not that they wouldn't have enjoyed the sampling.

But the disappointment after would have been worse than what they were experiencing now.

At the door to the vampire's condo, they paused and inhaled. There was no indication he had come back, nor one of his minions. Damien hoped like hell when the being did return, he would enjoy the calling card Luke and he left for him. Fucker should have known better than to come into their town and not let them know. There were rules for a reason. It kept the pissing contests down to a minimum. Damien and Luke had to show whoever the upstart was, they were the only ones allowed to piss on this side of the Missouri and Kansas border.

Chapter Four

Kellen was aware when the twins left the building. The air of power shrunk to where he didn't need to be as on edge, his wolf growled, the urge to shift riding him. "How did you shift when you needed to?" He tossed the bloody rag into her hamper.

"I shifted here in the apartment and sorta roamed around inside until she settled."

Laikyn wouldn't look him in the eyes.

He used his finger to lift her chin up. "That had to be hard. On the both of you. Why, Laikyn?" His hand kept her from dropping her chin to her chest.

Her chin wobbled. "After that night, I couldn't stay and watch you be with other women, knowing you didn't want me."

He'd screwed up so much that night. For years he tried to keep that side of his life separate from the Iron Wolves club, although the women he screwed were usually up for whatever he did to them. He liked to go to the clubs that catered to the lifestyle. BDSM. Never had he envisioned Laikyn in one of the clubs, especially up in Sioux Falls, a place he'd escape to many times. He wasn't even sure how she'd gotten into The Falls. The club's exclusive membership was one of the main reasons he had joined. They were part of a larger network of clubs, with subsidiaries in just about every major city in the country. You wouldn't know it was a place where debauchery of every kind lurked behind the closed doors from the outside. Hell, he was still in awe at the elegant remodeled old mansion. All the clubs that were linked were old estates that were turned into clubs. No pop-up shops, or renovated garage type buildings.

"Mon Chaton, I fucked up. I was running just as fast as my two, or four, legs would carry me back then. I thought I'd give you a few more years to grow up, then come hell or high water I was coming to claim you."

She snorted. "Yeah right. That's why the next day you had what's her name bouncing on your dick in your office."

Kellen growled. "I didn't have anybody on my cock the next day. For fucksake, you broke my dick for months." He caged her in when she tried to hop down.

"Bullshit. I saw it with my own eyes. I came by to talk with you, but you were sitting on one of the couches," she stopped, sucked in a breath, and tried to push him back. "But sitting like the king of all, right there on your big leather chair was you, with a human on your lap. She had her skirt hiked up, while your hands were massaging her ass, moaning endearments. I didn't stay around to watch the show, thank you very fucking much."

He screwed his eyes shut, trying to remember the next day. He remembered the drive back. The second fifth of whiskey. The third and fourth were a blur, but he knew for a fact his dick hadn't rose to the occasion until the smell of Laikyn had faded enough for his wolf to stop whining. Even then he had to truly work in order to get hard. "If you saw a chick on my lap, I can guarantee you that was as far as it got. My body wouldn't respond to anyone for over six goddamn months. I waited for you to return. Hell, I even called your parents in Florida until I am sure they were ready to change their number. Did they never tell you?"

"I can't believe that. I mean… you always had a female. Even that night… with me, it was, intense to say the least."

Kellen laughed. The sound hollow to his own ears. "You were strapped to a St. Andrew's Cross, getting ready to be whipped by a stranger. The sight had me and my wolf foaming at the mouth. It took all my self-control not to rip his arms off and beat him with them. When I released you, and heard you ask me to show you what I liked." He took a deep breath. "That you were there to learn how to please me, I swear to all, my heart broke. Not because I didn't already want you, but because I wasn't worthy of that. Of you. Don't you see, Mon

Chaton? You are my one weakness. My one and only true temptation that I can't walk away from."

She raised auburn brows. "You did a pretty damn good job the next day."

Scrubbing his hands down his face, he felt the stubble from the day's beard. "You were a virgin. A sweet little virgin, and to have taken you like I did." Laikyn covered his mouth with hers.

"You made my first, and so far, my last, special." Her green eyes sparkled up at him.

"I want to make love to you good and proper, but I don't think we have time." He looked about the large master bath. "You need to put on a clean top, while we get the rest of your stuff packed. From what Damien said we should be out of here before the sun sets, and while I'm not scared of a vampire, I'm not about to put you at risk. But baby, when I get you home, all bets are off."

The red flush that covered her face, and down into the opening of her shirt made him ache to see just how far down it went. Memories of their one night together had him hard as stone.

"Hurry up before I change my mind and say screw the fact our pack would hear you screaming my name." Yeah, he truly loved watching her blush.

"You say the dirtiest things," she said.

"If memory serves me correctly, you loved every second of it." He lifted her off the counter, stopping any protest with a deep searing kiss. Her arms and legs wrapped around him while he walked them back into her bedroom. At the edge of her bed, he stopped walking. With monumental effort he made himself stop kissing Laikyn. Her taste as addictive and fine as the best bourbon he owned. When her arms and legs relaxed, he let her fall softly to the mattress.

"I'm going to send Syn and Lyric in here to help you pack. What do you need us menfolk to do?"

A somewhat dazed look stared back at him for a second, then she smiled. "Menfolk, huh. How about if you guys start stacking the boxes I have already packed, and then when we finish, we can take down a bunch at a time?"

He noticed she'd already began packing and nodded. "Alright. Hurry up."

"Yes, Sir, Alpha Sir."

Knowing she wasn't expecting it, he flipped her onto her tummy and gave her a swat on her firm ass. "Keep it up and I'll add up all the times you made me jackoff."

Laikyn rolled back over. The arousal clear in her scent. "Promise?"

Fuck him, she was so his.

Kellen walked out without saying another word, fearing he'd jerk those leggings down and turn her ass red before fucking them both numb.

Lyric and Syn were closing up boxes while Rowan and Bodhi were stacking them near the door. He shook his head. "Lake asked if you ladies would help her finish up in her room and the bathroom while we did the grunt work rounding up the already packed boxes. It looks like you guys were way ahead of us though."

Rowan nodded. "Wasn't sure how long you'd be. Figured we'd get to work. No use wasting daylight if you know what I mean."

"Oh, real subtle, Ro," Lyric growled. She sealed the box she was working on. "Let's go, Syn, so the men can talk." She made air quotes.

"You really need to teach her who is in charge, Ro." Kellen swatted Lyric and Syn on the rear as they walked by. He'd been doing the same since they were little girls, but not like the love tap he gave Laikyn. With her, he wanted to strip her bare and have his way in every imaginable dirty way and soothe the redness with his lips and tongue.

"Yeah, I think I like my balls right where they are." Rowan picked up two boxes, carrying them near the door with the others.

They worked for the next couple hours until Laikyn had everything packed, marked and ready to load onto the trailer and in the truck.

"You gonna miss living here," Syn asked while the guys were picking up the last of the boxes.

Kellen froze, wondering what she would say.

"I'll miss working at the hospital here, but I think Mercy will be just as nice if not better since I'll be closer to my family and friends. I only took the residency here because it just happened to come up the day after... well it just came at the right time," she said on a gush of air.

"She will never get so far away from me again," Kellen growled.

Syn rolled her eyes. "Hello, she is getting away from two stalkerish dudes, no need to get all stalkerish yourself, brother dear."

"I can't wait to see you when you're claimed." He looked at Bodhi out of the corner of his eye, watching the male he considered a brother fidget with his cell phone. He'd noticed he'd been doing a whole lot of texting lately and made a mental note to ask him about it later.

It took even less time to carry the boxes down once they procured a cart, and then they stood next to the two large vehicles. Kellen didn't want to be separated from Laikyn for the next ten hours and could see she didn't either.

"Syn, have you ever driven a trailer loaded down with that much weight?" Rowan asked, rocking back on his heels.

His sister looked at her beloved black truck and then at the big man. She chewed on her lip, then glanced at the trailer loaded down, and the back of the pickup with more boxes.

"Come on, you know I'll treat her right. Besides, you'll be in the vehicle with me." Rowan held his hand out.

At that moment Kellen wanted to hug Rowan, maybe even promise to name his first born after him.

Syn placed the keys with the large, bedazzled heart keychain attached in his palm. "Fine, but I get to drive your truck sometime."

Rowan looked like a deer in the headlights at Syn's statement, which had Lyric laughing. Kellen glanced at Bodhi. "You riding with us or them." He pointed at the bickering Rowan and Syn.

"I'll ride with them. Give you two a little alone time. Pretty sure I'd gag from all the mushy vibes you'd be letting off in an enclosed vehicle."

Rubbing the side of his nose with his middle finger, Kellen helped Laikyn into the passenger side, before rounding the front. He raised his head as he felt a swell of power. The sun hadn't set, yet an unholy presence was waking. "Let's roll," he said forcefully, tapping the top of the XV before sliding in.

As he left the underground garage, the niggling in the back of his mind didn't abate until they hit the highway heading north. He assumed the Cordell brothers were checking up on them to make sure they made it out. He made a mental note to give them a call. The fact there were others as they called themselves meant he needed to find out more. Kellen wanted his pack to be prepared for any situation. Like Rowan had mentioned before, not everyone lived within the club. Many going off to college and finding homes away from the pack itself. Forewarned is forearmed, was his motto.

"You're awfully quiet." Laikyn's elegant hand reached for his.

"Could you tell anything was different about your coworkers?" He asked, taking his eyes off the road.

Laikyn took the hair band out, sifting her fingers through the red length. He watched her mull over his words before answering. "Honestly, no. I mean they always wore so much cologne. Which clearly was to mask their shifter side. But even now, knowing they are vampires, I have no clue how we would know."

He entwined their fingers. "I could feel a swell of power. I don't know if I could teach you and the others how to search for it. I am going to call them and ask for their help. Surely, they wouldn't have offered if they didn't mean it."

"Even though I didn't want to be the cream to their sandwich, they were great guys. I mean like the walk the little old ladies across the street, toss their jackets over puddles sort. I would almost bet my last nickel they were sincere." She ran her thumb over his.

He didn't smell one bit of lust for the Cordell brothers rolling off of her. "We'll talk about it tomorrow or the next day. You tired?"

"No. You?"

Kellen could go days without a full night's sleep. Now that Laikyn was with him, he didn't plan to fully rest until he had her settled in his bed. Preferably after he buried himself deep within her a few times. His dick twitched in agreement.

"Not in the least," he said.

Laikyn enjoyed the easy banter she and Kellen shared on the long ride back to South Dakota. Oh, she knew once they were back on his home turf, he'd become the big bad alpha she accused him of. The anticipation zinging through her veins was a slow simmer.

They stopped in the middle of Nebraska in the city of Omaha. Laikyn got out, stretching her legs.

She looked back at Syn and swore the other female wasn't the same as the one who'd driven her up the day before. The big dark blond male paced away from the group, his phone to his ear as he murmured to someone on the other end.

"What's going on with them?" She pointed to Kellen's sister Syn.

Kellen shrugged; his gaze trained on Bodhi. "He can't get his head out of his ass."

"Sounds like someone I know," she murmured to herself.

She watched as the male she loved stomped over to his sister. Laikyn leaned against the side of his vehicle and waited, her legs enjoying the comfort of standing upright. A breeze blew a lock of her hair across her face, tickling her nose. Using both hands she pulled the heavy mass of hair back into a loose ponytail at the back of her head.

The feeling of being watched made her look around, but other than a few men who looked more interested in Kellen's XV than her, she didn't notice anyone staring at her. Marking it down as left-over paranoia, she waited for the rest of the crew.

Minutes later Syn strolled up to where she stood. "I swear, my brother is going to be the reason I leave the Iron Wolves for good."

Laikyn watched the younger female's lazy walk as she entered the truck stop. She wanted to eat a real meal, and not something they heated up in a microwave, but she also wanted to get back to Kellen's place and finish what they'd started. Syn didn't seem to feel the same way, bypassing the frozen foods, and headed into the restaurant attached.

"I swear that girl is gonna give me grey hair." Kellen pulled Laikyn into his arms.

Looking over her shoulder, she smiled. "You'd look sexy with a little hint of silver at the temples."

Kellen pressed his hips against her ass. "I'll show you sexy when I get you alone. Come on, let's see what kind of trouble my sis is trying to get into."

Rowan and Lyric walked next to them, but she noticed Bodhi hadn't come back to the vehicle. "Where's Bodhi?"

The arm around her tightened for a second. "His phone seems to be blowing up, which in turn is making Syn madder than hell. Fuck, I wish he'd tell me what is going on, but all I get is 'not your problem', which is not like him at all." Kellen and Rowan made sure she and Lyric were sandwiched between them at all times, making her get a warm feeling in all the right places.

"He'll tell you when he's ready." Laikyn tried to reassure him. They found Syn seated at a large table, a drink in front of her.

"Syn, we want to get home sooner, rather than later." Kellen glared.

Taking a drink before answering, Syn motioned to the spaces around her. "Let's eat. I'm famished, and if I have to ride with that asshat, I need food."

"You can ride with Lake and me," Kellen growled.

"Of course, I can," Syn agreed.

Laikyn could see the storm was brewing and decided to sit down before they started an argument. Lyric clearly knowing her best friend was sliding in beside her first. The half-moon booth gave them plenty of room. Once they ordered breakfast an awkward silence descended. One that was marked by the absence of Bodhi.

The cheery waitress brought over the plates, which everyone dug into, but that eerie feeling of eyes on her had Laikyn whipping her head around.

"What's wrong, Mon Chaton?" Kellen reached for her hand.

Cold clammy tendrils snaked through her. "I feel as though someone, or something is watching me."

Kellen raised his head and breathed deeply.

Their plates were mostly empty, but she couldn't eat another bite if she wanted to.

"I smell nothing aside from the food, diesel fuel, humans, and gasoline. Let's pay the bill and get back on the road. You'll feel better once we're home." He raised his hand for the check.

Laikyn thought the little twenty something looked a little too eager to touch him as she reached for his card, making her wolf want to bite. He let out a gruff laugh, his hand smoothing over her thigh under the table, tracing up the inside of her leg. Just as the waitress was coming back, Kellen turned so his back was to everyone except Laikyn.

"Mon Chaton, I can't wait to slide my dick into your pussy. I've been hard as steel just thinking of the perfection that is you." His lips covered hers, silencing any words she might have said. His fingers reached their destination at the apex of her thighs making her moan.

"If you could sign this, please," the waitress said loudly.

And just like that, her wolf calmed. Kellen didn't look at the cute little blonde as he signed the check. His blue stare fixed directly on her, letting Laikyn know he meant every delicious word.

"Yeah, like I plan to ride in the vehicle with all that. Can I order a taxi back, or hop a plane? Hell, I bet there's a trucker going North," Syn muttered.

"You will ride with me, or Rowan in your vehicle. Your childish antics are over, Syn. You need to grow up and stop running away from them." Kellen slid from the booth, holding his hand out for Laikyn.

She watched Rowan do the same for Lyric, feeling sorry for Syn. Bodhi was keeping something from all of them. Laikyn knew it had to hurt, knowing the male you wanted wasn't being upfront with all that was going on in his life.

"Come on, Syn. You can ride with us. I'll even ride in the back so you and your brother can sit up front and do sibling stuff." Laikyn weaved her arm through Syn's with one of hers, keeping Kellen connected on her other side. He'd stiffened for a brief moment but relaxed in the next.

"You are too sweet, and way too delusional. Rowan and Lyric are at least somewhat calmed down from the mating lust after their time together. You two on the other hand, are just getting started. Nope, I'll just go torment Bo." Syn stood on her tiptoes and kissed her on the cheek. "Thank you for the offer, though."

Laikyn nodded. "We only have a few more hours and then we're home."

Syn gave them a false smile that didn't reach her eyes.

Bodhi reclined against Syn's truck. A paper bag gripped in his hand. The scents of microwaved burritos wafted from the package.

"How was your snack?" Syn asked with a glare.

"I thought y'all were coming right back?" Bodhi looked at each of them.

Kellen shrugged. "We decided to eat in. Why didn't you come inside?"

The big male stomped over to the trash and tossed his garbage away. "I didn't realize you weren't coming back until after I'd bought that junk and eaten a couple. Thanks for letting me know." He swung up into the vehicle without another word.

Rowan looked from Kellen to Bodhi and back. "You didn't do your mind talking thing with him?"

Kellen raised his middle finger. "Let's roll. I want to be home by sunrise. My skin itches."

Laikyn's did too, but she didn't think it was from lack of moisturizer. Again, she felt like someone, or something was watching her. However, she looked around the parking lot, but saw nothing out of place. The truck drivers all seemed normal. Families filled up the vehicles, or couples were busy doing the same. Still, the lingering sense that she was being followed didn't abate until she hopped up into Kellen's vehicle. She buckled in, and manually locked the door.

"Hey, you're safe with me, Mon Chaton. I will kill anyone or anything that tried to harm a hair on your delectable body." He ran a palm over her head, freeing her hair from the tie. "I love your hair down. It's like the color of the setting sun with all its reds shining. I can't wait to see it fanned out on my pillows."

"You say these things just to get me to blush. Don't you?" She bit her bottom lip.

He leaned over, taking her bottom lip into his mouth. "Well, you do it so beautifully. I just can't help myself."

A loud horn interrupted them.

"I seriously am going to have to kick that man's ass," Kellen said starting his vehicle and backing out.

Chapter Five

Kellen truly did like Rowan. He was sure the other male was born a shifter, he just needed to be bitten to become one. He had absolutely no fear, or respect for him as alpha, which Kellen sort of respected. While they drove along, he reached out to Bodhi through their link, making sure he kept the others from overhearing. *"Yo, Bodhi. What's going on?"*

"Nothing, man. I just got some shit I need to deal with. I'm gonna need to scat for a couple weeks when we get back. I'll keep in touch, but there's some things I need to take care of."

"Speak to me. Tell me what it is, and I'll help. You know pack is always here for one another."

The silence that stretched was deafening.

"It's not pack, and I'm just gonna leave it at that." Bodhi's deep growl came through the link as did his worry.

Kellen decided not to push at the moment.

"Bodhi's gonna break your sister's heart." Laikyn's observation startled him.

He wasn't sure if she had read his thoughts, or if she was thinking out loud, or if Syn and she had talked while they'd been together. The first option disturbed him, making his next words come out harsher than he'd planned. "What do you know about it?"

Laikyn jerked as if he'd slapped her. "I know how it feels to have a male reject you."

Seeing her cross her arms, the move one of defense, like she worried he'd reach over and grab her made his wolf howl inside him. Neither of them liked seeing their mate upset, especially when she was putting up a wall between them. Kellen wouldn't allow her to shut down on them, even if it was his fault. He reached for one of her hands, the cold fingers startling to him.

"I'm sorry, Mon Chaton. I didn't mean to snap at you. When I asked how you knew about Bodhi and Syn, I meant to ask if she'd talked about them. I wasn't trying to be an ass." He rubbed his thumb back and forth, enjoying the softness of her skin. Damn, he could just imagine what it would feel like having her palm rubbing along his shaft.

Laikyn eyed him warily. "You are an ass, though." Her eyes lost some of their sadness.

Kellen brought their linked hands to his mouth, placing a kiss against her knuckles. "You keep talking like that, and I'll have to punish you. You do know how I like to punish little girls, don't you?"

Carnal heat suffused the vehicle. He could see she no longer thought of cutting him in half but was still unsure of them. He'd have to convince her he wasn't the big asshole she thought he was. Of course, he was the alpha, and as such his word was law. But Kellen liked to believe he did make exceptions to every rule, and that included how he ran the pack. That didn't mean he'd allow anyone to talk back to him without some form of punishment. He'd just make Laikyn's a little more pleasure than pain. Something they'd both take great enjoyment from. His dick jerked in agreement.

"I haven't been little for a long time." She smiled, her eyes daring him.

His body wanted to show her who was in charge in the worst way possible. The only thing stopping him from pulling over, was the fact they had a vehicle with four members of his pack following behind. Otherwise, Kellen was sure he'd already have his dick buried somewhere inside Laikyn.

"Next to me you're tiny. Now, behave or I'll have to pull over and show you just how little you are." He placed their entwined hands on his upper thigh, not quite touching the erection straining to get out.

The stunning creature wiggled her fingers until they were lying flat, inching her way up higher until she was touching the bulge he couldn't hide. "Why, I do declare, Mr. Styles. Is that a pickle in your pocket? Or are you glad to see me?"

As her fingers trailed up and down the jean covered length, Kellen grit his teeth. "I'm pretty sure pickles don't come in that size."

"I'm pretty sure pickles don't come." The way she said the words and the sparkle in her green eyes attested to the naughty girl inside his mate.

"You keep stroking that one, and it will… damn it, female, you're killing me here." Kellen swore he hadn't been that turned on by a female rubbing his shaft since he'd first started fooling around with the opposite sex.

"I want to touch you. Will you let me?" Laikyn asked as she reached for his belt buckle.

Goddess save him, but Kellen couldn't have stopped her from undoing it if they were in rush hour traffic and surrounded by a busload of school kids. He needed to feel her skin on him.

The top button came undone, then the excruciating slowness of each tine separating seemed to take forever. When she had his zipper completely open and his dick was able to unfold from the confines of his briefs, Kellen was sure his eyes crossed.

"Damn, I forgot how big you were." Her hand ran up and down from the tip to where the jeans stopped her.

"I'm the perfect size for you, baby." It was a tight fit, but he always could make it work.

Laikyn leaned over the console, her mouth hovering over his, but not blocking the view of the road. "Can you drive, while I suck you off?"

Kellen nearly ran them off the road at her question. "God damn. Warn a male before you say things like that."

Laikyn's husky laugh had his cock jerking, precome leaking from the tip. Her index finger swiped over the pearly fluid, rubbing it back and forth. "I have great faith you won't kill us."

With those words, her head bent and then Kellen was sure he'd blow his load in three seconds' flat. Her mouth was like the sweetest torture a male could have, the warm wet suction had him lifting his hips in time with her motions.

He kept a white-knuckle grip on the steering wheel with one hand, while the other he tunneled into her fiery mass of hair.

"Shit, your mouth is like fucking heaven." It took all his concentration to stay on the road. Shit, he was sure he crossed over the center line a time or two. Luckily the highway was empty save for their two vehicles.

Laikyn hummed around him, adding to the assault on his senses. He felt his balls draw up. His fingers tightened around the strands in his fist. "Mon Chaton, I'm about two seconds from coming down your throat."

Her head tilted, and the green eyes that mesmerized him, blinked lazily up at him while she licked the tip of his shaft. "That was my plan, Alpha Sir."

Kellen barely kept his beast from roaring. Was sure his wolf was wanting to claim their mate, the need to shift and do just that was almost like the first time he'd shifted as a boy.

Laikyn turned her focus back to licking and sucking him, using her hand to work the part of his cock she couldn't take. One day Kellen planned to train her to take all of him down her throat.

The squeeze and twist motion she applied in tandem with her sucking brought him to the edge. Although he wanted it to last, he knew he couldn't and stay sane. The first shot of come was like the first time he'd experienced an orgasm as a kid. Kellen heard himself yell but couldn't say what. His eyes bounced from the road, back to the red-haired vixen who greedily sucked him till he had nothing else to give, then lovingly licked him until he was clean.

"You taste good," she murmured, smacking her lips together.

With a growl, Kellen jerked the vehicle to the side of the road, coming to a rocking halt and hauled Laikyn into his lap. He covered her lips with his, kissing the sweet temptress like a starving man.

They broke apart at the sound of knocking on the passenger window, his wolf nor the male happy with the interruption. Luckily, Laikyn was covering his lap, and the fact his dick was out for all to see.

From inside he could see Rowan standing with a knowing smirk on his face. Lowering the window, Kellen waited for the other man to speak.

"Yeah, so just wanted to know if we should maybe give y'all a few, or if you were done playing tonsil hockey or you know?"

Kellen raised his right hand, middle finger extended. "Sit and spin, soldier boy."

Rowan laughed, walking back to the truck behind them.

Laikyn buried her face in his neck. "I didn't think I'd like that so much. Now, I really want to do it again."

Banging his head against the soft headrest, Kellen had to remind himself why it was not a good idea to let her. For one, he'd probably wreck, and for two, he'd definitely pull over again, and next time he'd have his mate's pants down and either his face buried between her thighs, or his cock. Either way, he was sure the four behind him wouldn't be amused. Or, they'd be amused, and he'd have to hurt them. Kellen couldn't hurt the women. Therefore, he'd make the men suffer twice as bad. Then, he'd be the bad guy.

"You realize when you think really hard you get two lines right here?" Laikyn traced between his brows.

He caught her hand in his. "Female, you are a menace to society."

With ease, he placed her back into the passenger seat. "You say the nicest things." Laikyn buckled up.

Kellen tucked himself back into his jeans, wishing the trip was over. As he watched, a shiver wracked Laikyn's frame. "Are you cold?"

She ran her hands up and down her arms. "Have you ever heard the saying about someone just stepped over your grave?"

Kellen hung his hand over the wheel and stared at Laikyn, unsure how to answer her. He was sure he didn't like the thought that someone would be anywhere near Laikyn, especially if they had plans to hurt her. He couldn't imagine a life where she wasn't in it. Knowing the saying meant someone had walked over the place she would someday be laid to rest, made all his inner warnings flare to life. He opened his senses, searching for the unknown, but didn't get anything other than he and Laikyn. "Let's just get home. You are going to outlive me, or I'll tan your hide."

"That sounds like a promise," she said leaning closer to his side.

If it wasn't for the console separating them, he knew without a doubt she'd be snuggled up next to him.

Laikyn didn't want to freak out, but the same eerie feeling she'd had at her apartment flared as she and Kellen had been sitting alongside the road. She believed it wasn't her two ex-co-workers, but fear of the unknown was much worse. The fact she had no clue they were part vampire, and couldn't sense, or smell them, worried her. She trusted

Kellen to protect her, but how could you protect against something you didn't know was there? Hell, she'd never seen the man who lived across the hall. If she had, she didn't remember. Making a mental note to call Damien and Luke to find out more first chance she got let her relax and enjoy the rest of the trip.

Kellen let her choose what they listened to on the radio, shocking her. They both enjoyed the same type of music. Their choices ranged from rock to newer country, and even classic rock. He said he got all stabby when pop music came on, which made her laugh.

"So, you don't like the Biebs?" Laikyn asked on a yawn.

"The who?" Kellen signaled for their exit.

Laughing she turned the radio up on the song with the artist in question. "I think he has the voice of an angel."

The big bad alpha rolled his eyes. "I'd snap his ass in two with one hand."

She snorted. "Of course, you can. But can you sing like that," she asked nodding toward the radio.

"Nope. Don't need to. I can fuck like a machine. He can sing all night long. Whereas I can fuck all night long. I call that a win win. I'll take my expertise over his any day."

His words had her squirming. She watched him inhale, the blue of his eyes turned brighter.

"I can smell you. The taste of you is still fresh in my mind. Would you like to listen to him sing while I'm buried deep inside you, Mon Chaton?"

And just like that, she was ready to leap over the seat and have her wicked way with him. "You are making me a right hussy, you know that? I mean, seriously. I think I've thought of sex like a dozen times in the past two years, and each time was when I thought of you. I've thought of nothing but sex since I saw you again."

He ran his hand up her inner thigh, stopping between and pressing. "I bet you are wet."

Laikyn didn't even think of lying. "Of course, I am."

The lights from the Iron Wolves Club were lit up with the parking lot full of cars and trucks, and a multitude of bikes. Kellen continued driving till he reached the back lot where the apartments were located. Disappointment hit her that he hadn't taken her, and the trailer filled with her belongings directly to his place.

"I need to stop here for a few, then we'll head home. We'll store the trailer in my barn. Do you want to come inside with me or wait out here?"

She wondered if he'd read her mind. Her walls were up with no signs of cracks in her mind. Even the twins couldn't breach them, which coming from hybrids was obviously quite the feat.

"I better call my parents and let them know I'm back. I'll meet you inside in a few."

Kellen leaned over and kissed her quick and hard. "If you're not there by the time I finish, I'll come back. It shouldn't take more than ten, maybe fifteen minutes."

He hopped out, striding back to the other vehicle. Rowan and Lyric stayed inside with Syn,

119

but Bodhi hopped out, a scowl on his face. Laikyn opened her door and walked back to speak to the others. "What's up with Bodhi?"

Syn shrugged her shoulders. "No effing clue. He was silent most of the trip, save for some tapping on his phone. If I didn't know better, I'd say he had a mate somewhere."

Hurt flashed across the gorgeous younger female's features. Laikyn stood on the running board. "Don't do what I did and run away for years. You don't want to lose two years of your life. Trust me on that."

"Hey, it's no biggie. Rowan, you guys think you can handle unloading and all that, then bring my rig to me tomorrow? I'll catch a ride home with one of my friends inside. I could use a drink or twenty." Syn's smile didn't reach her eyes.

"Let Kellen know, but yeah, I got this." Rowan agreed.

"Thank you. Take care of my girl. Oh, and Lyric too." Syn hopped down.

Laikyn watched her friend walk through a door farther down than the one Bodhi entered.

"She going to be, okay?" Laikyn asked Lyric, knowing the two girls were best friends.

Lyric looked sad. "She will be once one stupid wolf gets his head out of his ass. I just hope he does it before she does something that can't be taken back."

"Darlin, if you know something that I should, you better tell me." Rowan's deep growl reminded her of his presence.

"I promise, if I know she's in danger, I'll scream it from the rooftops. Right now, she just needs to get wasted and blow off some steam." Lyric patted her mate's leg.

"Who needs to get wasted?" Kellen asked.

Laikyn nearly screamed at Kellen's deep baritone so close to her ear. She hadn't heard him come up behind and wondered if the others hadn't either. From the shock on Lyric and Rowan's face she assumed Kellen had indeed snuck up on all three of them. "You almost made me pee my pants, Kellen."

He nuzzled her neck. "Hmm, that is not how I want to get your panties wet."

"TMI, boys and girls. You ready to roll? I need to practice making babies," Rowan said.

Kellen glared at Rowan. "Don't you already know how to do that? Do I need to give you a tutorial or what? You take part A, and stick it into part B. You need more instructions, like a video? I have several of those as well." Kellen's arms wrapped around her middle while he joked with Rowan.

Lyric laughed. "I think we know the how, it's just fun practicing until we are actually ready to do the making. Of course, if you are volunteering for babysitting duty, we might just step up the timeframe," she said blinking up at Kellen.

Laikyn was lifted off her feet. "You watch your own brats. I'm going to go practice with Laikyn after we unload the stuff from the back of Syn's truck. Let's roll out."

Kellen carried her back to his XV and deposited her in the front seat. "I am all up for practicing with you, Mr. Styles."

"That is good to hear, since I plan to practice a whole hell of a lot. Buckle up, baby." He waited for her to do the seatbelt then shut the door.

"If you need instructions, remember I'm a doctor. I know all about anatomy." She winked as he paused in starting the vehicle.

"You really are mounting up those spanks."

And didn't that just make all her girly parts tingle. She wondered just how far she'd let him go and couldn't wait to find out. Laikyn knew Kellen wouldn't hurt her in any way. A nice, sensual spanking though? Yeah, she totally thought she'd be down for that.

"What's put that look on your face, and got you all hot and bothered," Kellen asked with one hand on the wheel, the other placed possessively on her thigh.

Even if she wanted to lie, which she didn't, he'd smell her deceit. "I was just thinking of your hand on my ass." Hearing the words come out of her mouth had a visual that nearly had her squirming.

Kellen's fingers tightened on the wheel. "Me, too. Have you counted up the number yet? I think we should start at an even ten. What do you think?"

Damn! She thought of his big hand coming down on her backside. "What if I don't like it?"

Electric blue eyes turned to her. "You'll love it."

She didn't doubt his words and loved the deep growl that accompanied them. Lord, she couldn't wait to get to his place and explore.

"Wow, it's awfully foggy," she commented.

"Yeah! That it is." His head turned back and forth.

Laikyn glanced behind them to see if Rowan and Lyric were still following but couldn't see their headlights. "Should I call Lyric and make sure they're good? This fog sort of crept up on us."

He gave a sharp nod, slowing down as the heavy stuff clouded the view from the front.

As she pulled her phone out, the no signal sign glared at her. "My phone has no service. How about yours?"

Kellen pointed to his front pocket. At any other time, she'd be psyched at reaching in and teasing him. Now, she hoped his phone worked. Her heart pounded as she saw three bars. Quickly she dialed Lyric, waiting for the other female to answer.

"Hey, girl. Where did you two disappear to?" Lyric's voice had a note of fear.

"Put it on speaker," Kellen ordered.

Laikyn didn't know if he meant her or Lyric but did as he said.

"Where are you guys?" Kellen entered his address into the GPS, watching the screen on the dash.

"We're sitting outside your place. Y'all just sort of disappeared on us. We thought maybe you were taking her around the back of the property and would meet us around the front. What's going on?" Rowan kept his tone level.

"We were about a half a mile from my turn off when some heavy fog came in. I had my eyes peeled for the road but couldn't see shit. I'm at a crawl, man, but my wolf is itching to get out. The only reason I ain't is cause this rig is the safest place for Laikyn with me in it." Kellen reached for her hand.

"I'm going to call up her doctor friends. This doesn't sound natural. What did he say about that vamp across the hall?" Rowan asked.

Her body threatened to shake apart. Could vampires control the weather? "I don't know who he was. To my knowledge I never even met him," she swore.

"Calm down, Lake. We will figure this out. I'm going to call the twins on my phone while I keep you on this line."

Laikyn rattled off Damien's number, praying he'd answer an unknown call. The seconds that passed seemed like hours.

"Hello, wolfie. What's going on?" Damien's smug voice rang loud and clear.

"I will shove my wolf paw up your ass, spikey," Rowan growled.

Damien laughed. "Not my thing. How about you tell me why you're calling me?"

"Damien, it's me, Laikyn. Kellen and I were driving when fog rolled in so thick, we couldn't see. It separated us from Rowan and Lyric, and it's not normal fog, that much I can tell you." She hurried to say before Rowan and Damien got into a pissing contest.

The sound of her ex-partners voices whispering had her on edge. Kellen continued driving, although where they were going, she wasn't sure. From the GPS, it seemed they were a good three miles away from the road they should have taken.

"I know this is going to sound strange, and your mate is not going to like it, but you will need to listen and allow me to take over, Lake. Kellen, if you can hear me, which I'm sure you can, I am going to follow the path that is open through this call and find you and Laikyn. I would use you, but I fear you are too strong, and the struggle too great.

What I'm saying is I can be there through Laikyn. She will still be there as well, but I can help. I will be able to see what is creating the fog, and possibly counteract the spell. Once it is done, I will retreat, and leave your mate unharmed."

Laikyn looked at Kellen, the automatic no written on his gorgeous face. She put her fingers over his mouth, then motioned to the fog that kept getting thicker by the moment. "If we continue, we could drive off a cliff."

"Do it, Damien. However, if you harm one hair on her, I will hunt you down and you'll pray for death before I'm done with you."

"I don't doubt that for a moment, Alpha. Now, Laikyn, I need you to open your mind and relax as best you can," Damien murmured.

She closed her eyes, concentrating on breathing in and out. She even brought up a mental picture of Damien and his smirking face. A flood of power filled her, making her shrink into a ball at the back of her mind. *"Kellen, I think Damien is in my mind or whatever."*

"Yes, Mon Chaton. You're very brave. Stay calm, and we will get us out of here." She felt a ghost touch, like his fingers stroking down her cheek.

"Damn, I hate taking over a female's body. Alright, let's see what we got here. P.S. keep the line open cause baby bro is watching my body and listening in. Just in case I need assistance." Damien spoke through Laikyn's body, sounding like himself.

Chapter Six

Kellen wasn't one to freak out normally but hearing a man's voice come out of his mate, nearly did it for him. "Alright, do your thing and make it quick." He didn't care that he sounded ungrateful. The fact Laikyn was not present in the front of her mind was not something he or his wolf liked.

"This is definitely the work of a vamp, and not a young one either. I can't sense his presence, which means he is doing this from afar. Damn! Let me focus. You need to stop the vehicle, though. There is a drop-off around the corner, and I'm pretty sure you're not seeing it on the GPS thing properly, but I can see it."

Damien shoved the image into Kellen's mind. The invasion another thing Kellen wasn't happy with. He pulled to a stop, immediately noticing the swirling mass of smoke surround them. "Do your magic quick."

Laikyn's hands came up, moving in a fast pattern. Kellen looked back to the road, then at her hands. Minutes ticked by as silence reigned over them. His wolf rose to the front of his mind, needing to protect their mate. He wanted to reach out on their path and connect with her, wishing he'd claimed her properly, but promised himself they'd correct that oversight when this was over.

The grey smoke-like fog began to recede. Almost looking like tendrils of ropes, or ghostly fingers reaching for them, until finally the road was clearly visible. Laikyn's hands dropped, but the eyes staring out were the black orbs of Damien.

"It is done. Luke and I will search for him in Kansas City, but I fear he is on the hunt for you, and Laikyn. Somehow, he has caught her scent the same as my brother and I did. The big difference is, we have honor. This being doesn't. He was testing you both. I can arm you, so you will be able to sense when he is near, but you will need to trust me." Damien turned to stare at Kellen through Laikyn.

Knowing the immediate threat was gone, he reached for his mate in the back of her mind, wanted to reassure them both they were indeed fine. She appeared calm, but he sensed she wasn't at all.

Kellen nodded. "What do you need to do?" He wasn't going to agree to anything without being informed.

An image was thrust into his mind. Kellen allowed the invasion. The powerful hybrid filled him with more knowledge, which he was aware Laikyn was getting as well. Being able to sense an enemy was a must when they were used to being the predator. He created a link with Damien, the thin tie back to the other being, one only he would know about, until the time came that he'd need it. Kellen had a feeling they would need it in the coming battle.

"Magic such as we use is passed from generation to generation. My family is old, and from what I just undid, I can attest that we are far older than he. However, that doesn't make him less dangerous. Actually, it makes him unstable. For a vampire to be so focused on a female to such an extent is very dangerous. Had she been marked, I'm sure he'd have left her alone. But that is no longer something he cares about. Even if you were to mark her as yours, he will think she was open game. Meaning, he will take what he felt was his first."

"Thank you. You may leave my mate's body now, vamp." Kellen wanted to touch Laikyn, but not while another possessed her.

Laikyn's head bent in the regal way, then the black eyes blinked, becoming the green of hers. She shivered, running her hands up her arms. "That was way creepy."

He had to agree. "Let's get to my place and set safeguards like the vamps showed us. Did you catch all he said and pushed into my mind?" Kellen made a turn in the middle of the road, the maneuver taking several attempts to get turned around.

She nodded. "I did, although it was as if I was watching instead of being there. Definitely not something I want to do again."

133

Kellen saw goosebumps on her arms, wishing he could erase the last half hour.

"You realize I'm still here, right?" Damien's voice came over the phone.

"Motherfucker," Kellen growled.

"I'm sure I've done that a few times," Damien agreed, then sobered. "You both will need to be vigilant. The being will now know you had help, and maybe even rethink his pursuit." Kellen pictured the elegant man shrugging.

"I don't think any of us think he will actually do that, do we?" Kellen reached the road to his home, happy to see Rowan and Lyric waiting for them.

"Unfortunately, I don't think we've seen the last of him. But, since you so conveniently created a link with me... yes, I felt your presence, Alpha, you will always be able to contact me. Just try to knock first. I do like my privacy. Feel free to share what I taught you with your pack. Knowledge is power, wolfman." Damien ended the call before Kellen could say another word.

"What does he mean you created a link?" Laikyn asked.

Not wanting to discuss the vamps with her, he hit the opener to the garage door and pulled inside. Once he had them secure, Kellen pulled her onto his lap, kissing Laikyn as if he hadn't done so in days instead of hours. He didn't like to admit it, but the vampire attack worried him. If they hadn't had Damien's assistance, he wasn't sure what would have happened.

"You would have saved me," Laikyn said against his lips.

Her faith in him made him feel ten feet tall. "I'll always protect you. You come first, middle, and last in my world. My every waking breath will be filled with your scent. I need you, Laikyn."

"We should help Rowan unload the trailer into the barn for the night." Laikyn nuzzled against his neck.

She fit him. He called her his kitten, and the way she was rubbing up against him, the soft little sighs, he truly thought the name appropriate, even though they were wolves.

"Alright, let's get it done, so I can make you mine properly." Kellen opened his door, climbing out with Laikyn in his arms.

"It's a good thing you're such a big man, Kellen." Laikyn wrapped her arms around his neck.

He looked down at her. "Why's that," he asked letting her slide down the front of his body.

"You're always picking me up, and I'm far from a small chick." She stood on her toes and kissed his beard stubbled chin.

Kellen gripped her ass, bringing her flush with his hard-on. "Thank god for that. I love how you fit against me."

Banging on the door had him growling. "Damn that Rowan."

She laughed. "He is probably wanting to get home and practice making babies."

"Boy needs to figure that shit out," Kellen mumbled striding to the door.

At the door Rowan and Lyric stood with worried expressions. Rowan held his hand up, ready to knock again. "I know how to make babies. I just enjoy the practice. Tell her we are ready to do the making and it is game on. Now, what the fuck happened?"

They spent the next few minutes getting the trailer in the barn, then Kellen ushered the couple into the large log home. After he shared the information Damien had given them, Rowan began to pace.

"How do we protect the entire pack if he decides to pull the same shit on them that he did on you two?"

"Forewarned is forearmed, man. Besides, I can share with everyone at once." Kellen kept his tone level.

Lyric stood in front of Rowan. "He's the alpha, remember."

"So, do you send out a call or text?" Humor laced Rowan's voice, but Kellen saw through to the real worry.

Kellen nodded. "Something like that. I believe a mind-fuck some might call it, but I will do a little love tap first. I hate to bombard everyone at once, however it must be done now. I'm going to give Xan a heads up first." Kellen gave Laikyn a kiss. "You will have to ignore his snarly attitude."

"What do you mean?" Laikyn blinked up at him.

"I don't plan to keep you out, so when I tap on Xan's mind, he'll more than likely be snarling back at me. Ignore him."

Within minutes Kellen and Xan were mind-speaking, luckily, he and Breezy weren't in the process of doing the deed, making the snarling minimal. As Kellen's second, Xan would help Kellen funnel the information throughout the pack.

"I say we use Rowan and his link with Lyric as well. He's a strong alpha, not to mention a force to be reckoned with," Xan suggested.

Kellen looked at the big man. "You want to help spread the information, and reinforce the barriers?"

Rowan stood taller. "Absolutely."

Nigel Watson fell to his knees. Wielding that much power cost him dearly, especially from so far away. He'd tried trailing the wolves, but they'd left before he'd risen, making him curse the fact he couldn't walk in the day like those bastard twins. "I should hunt them down and kill them for their interference."

"Master, do you have need of me?" One of his feeders asked. The petite human knelt next to his sleeping chamber, head bent, exposing the pale column of her throat.

His teeth ached to bite into the flesh, take what he needed and to hell with the consequences. Modern day technology kept him from following through. Instead, he motioned her forward. She stood gracefully, the long silver gown one he'd chosen for all his feeders moved with each step she took. He swung around, spreading his legs, and watched as she fell to the hard stone between his knees. The sound of her blood flowing had him tugging her head to the side. Her soft moan had his cock springing to life, but he ignored that hunger until the other was sated.

Nigel swiped his tongue over the marks, making sure no signs were left behind. It wouldn't do him any good to have the world know of his existence. Although, he had contemplated pointing the police toward the Cordell brothers for a string of murders, but they were hybrids. Damn daywalkers could go out in the sun, something he hadn't been able to do since his turning in the early nineteen hundred. He was made, unlike them as well. Born vampires thought they were better than those who were created, but Nigel had killed his maker years ago, taking his powers into himself. In his mind that made him equal to those that were born.

A grin split his lips. He'd not stopped at taking his own maker's head. Hell, he'd lost count of the number of vamps heads he'd taken, making him one of the strongest, and seemingly oldest of their kind. He now craved something else. A female who loved him above all others.

"Do you require more of me, Master?"

Blue eyes stared up at him. He liked having his people below him. At only five feet eight, most men and some women towered over him. He nodded toward his lap. She stared at his erection. Again, he hated having to use his powers, but he made her want him. His mate would not need to have such things done to her mind. He'd seen the bond when a vampire found his Hearts Love and wanted one for himself. When the female shifter had applied for residency in his condo building, instantly he'd recognized she was different. However, it wasn't until the hybrid twins began sniffing around her, he'd realized she could be his one.

He guided her to where he wanted, imaging the red-haired Laikyn. Flashing green eyes replaced blue. Nigel wanted to last, but the thought of having the female shifter on her knees, at his mercy brought him off quickly. He kept his roar to himself, enjoying the feel of the soft tongue laving him till he was clean.

"Up you go. Tell Arie I will be there shortly."

She nodded, then was gone. If he had a heart, he'd feel bad for not giving her relief. Shrugging he stood, stretching. The fresh blood replenished him from the attempt at bringing Laikyn back to him.

"I'll just have to come to you, my dear." First, he'd have to deal with the Cordell twins, and find out exactly where she'd gone. He was looking forward to the coming confrontation. If luck were on his side, he'd kill one or both of them. Nigel hoped by taking their lives he'd also take on their power of daywalking. Or, if not, at least they would no longer be an obstacle in his life. When he bonds with Laikyn, he assumed he would then take on some of her abilities. Being a shifter or part shifter with his great powers would make him invincible. He'd then go back to the Council of Elders and take the head of the leader. "Nigel Watson, leader of all vampires sounds like a perfect title to me."

Walking naked to his large closet he surveyed his choice of clothing. Since becoming a vampire, he'd worked hard at making his body the best it could be. He could do nothing for his short stature, but not an ounce of flab could be found on him. Unlike how he'd looked over a hundred years ago. A growl escaped his throat as he pictured the pale faced youth he'd been. The images of the abuse and mistreatment he'd taken as a short, young man, had him seeing red. Nigel had gone back to the local area he'd grown up in, found the men who'd taken joy in beating up on the young, pimple faced kid Nigel had been. When he'd faced them at the local pub, they'd been shocked to see him standing before them dressed in his fine clothes, tailored to perfection. He'd had more muscles than all of them put together, but they'd still thought them better than him. A laugh bubbled out as he remembered the fear in their eyes. He'd challenged them to a fight. Four to one, and they were so smug. A crowd gathered to watch Nigel get his ass handed to him.

Jerking a red button-down shirt, and a pair of black slacks from the row in front of him, Nigel let his memory unfold to the end, where the four men where left lying in a puddle of their own blood. Their limbs in total abandon where he'd tossed their unconscious bodies on top of one another. The onlookers gave him a wide berth as he'd strolled through them. His knuckles were the only thing showing any damage. The murmurs from those who should have protected him, now raised in alarm from what he'd done to the clearly much larger men. Nigel shrugged into the clothing, using the powers that allowed him to clean himself without the need of modern technology. "Idiots, all of them. I should have killed the lot while I was there."

Nigel pulled his pants on, the anger still burned him as he remembered the mob that had come for him the following night. His master had been angry at Nigel for being *petty*, almost allowing him to be staked. It was in that moment that he'd decided he'd take Miles' head. It had taken him twenty years, but Nigel was patient, and learned from the best. Miles was a devious fucker who didn't deserve loyalty. Not a day went by that Nigel regretted his choice to end Miles. Being a slave to a master was not a comfortable place to be. Especially when you were completely heterosexual but forced to serve a man who didn't care. He shuddered, blocking the years he was forced to do whatever Miles said in order to survive.

"I'm a much better master than you, Miles Jordan." And he was. He didn't take men. Only women.

Using the private elevator that only he and his feeders had access to, Nigel went up to the ground floor of the condo building. The condo he'd been using across the hall from Laikyn was now empty as was hers. He cursed the twins again for running her off. It all came back to them.

"Good evening, Master. What would you require of me this evening?" Arie stood in a black evening dress with a red belt cinching her tiny waist. A pair of red high heels, with her hands folded in front of her, she looked the part of a sexy woman, and perfect hostess. All the things he enjoyed in a personal assistant. Plus, she knew exactly what he was.

"I need to find out where Laikyn has gone, and I want the Cordell twins' heads on a platter. The first you can do, the latter I'll take care of myself."

He heard her heartrate kick up a notch. His assistant never failed him, but he wondered what caused her to react the way she had. He tried to look into her mind, but the block caused him to recoil. "Do you have a problem, Arie?"

Arie shook her head. She'd been sent to keep watch over Nigel from the Vampire Council. As one of the only other hybrids, her job was to appear human. For over three years she'd been his perfect companion. Yet, not once had she seen him outright kill anyone. She hadn't understood why the Council had sent her, a young hybrid in the world of their kind, but didn't question them. Of course, she'd heard of the Cordell twins.

Everyone who was anyone had. Pulling her mind back to Nigel, she pasted a serene smile on her face. "No, master. I will get on the first issue.

I'm sure we have her information from when she applied for residency to live here. I'll get on it now. Will there be anything else?"

Nigel's head tilted, the slight balding on the top glinted in the overhead lights. If he wasn't evil to the core, she was sure he'd be found attractive, especially with all his muscles. Although she preferred her men to be tall and blond. Why she had a thing for men who resembled Thor, she had no clue, but he just did it for her.

"That will be all for now," Nigel said. "Oh, and Arie," he paused. "Do make haste." Nigel's dark eyes bore into her.

Arie nodded. "Consider it done. Will you be in need of any more feeders this evening?" She glanced over at the young female she'd sent down earlier. Carly was young and easily able to manipulate. However, Arie wouldn't be sending the young female back to Nigel for at least a week.

"I will get my own sustenance this evening. I've already partook of the female you sent down, but

I'll be sure to take my fill before sunset. Have something for me before I return."

Nigel stomped out of the large apartment. His usual smooth gait gone. Arie worried he was on to her but shook off the doubt. She'd have to be more reserved and hide her feelings on the Cordell brothers. No way could he harm either of them, no matter how powerful he was. Fear for them plagued her as she made her way to the manager's office. The Council had given her strict instructions to inform them if Nigel did anything they needed to know about, and up until that moment she had nothing to truly report, except for the first time she'd been inducted into his world. That night still gave her nightmares. Before she could talk herself out of it, Arie opened the link to the head of the Council, sharing the conversation she'd had with her boss.

"Thank you for your bravery, young Arie. My sons are very lucky to have you watching over them. Now, you must return to us. It is too dangerous for you to stay there." A female's voice Arie assumed

was Mrs. Cordell entered her head, making her stop in her tracks.

Arie looked around, feeling as if she should curtsy or kneel. The royal was one who she'd never expected to speak with, let alone have a private conversation. *"Your highness, with all due respect, my job is not done here. I believe I would be more useful here watching within, than to leave now. Nigel trusts me, and as such, I can keep an eye on him."*

"Youth are so foolish. He will kill you if he discovers you are not on his side. You are too important to our people."

"Miss Black, what my Hearts Love is saying is, we appreciate your information. I will of course keep a close eye on the situation at hand. Thank you for your service. Now, we need you to return home so we can be assured of your safety."

Her knees shook at the authoritative voice of the head of the Vampire Council. The Cordell twin's father was none other than the male who sent her to watch over them. She looked around the manager's office, wondering what she was doing there. *"I'm supposed to help Nigel locate a female named Laikyn. I'm afraid he'll lose his shit... sorry, I'm afraid he will go a little crazy if I don't give him the information he has requested."*

"I'll handle it. You need to get out of there. I've got men coming to back you and my sons up. Mr. Watson is not stable."

"Okay, I'll make it look as though I've searched in case he checks. I'll need to get the humans out of the apartment. His feeders as he calls them, or he may take it out on them." Arie wouldn't take the chance a human would be injured or killed because of her.

A feminine sigh whispered through her mind. The feeling of fingers stroking her cheek soothed her frayed nerves. *"You are more precious than you give yourself credit for."*

Arie swallowed a lump in her throat. Having lost both her parents in a fire years before, she'd been grateful the Council had taken her in and allowed her to live under their care. Being a hybrid had set her aside from both her heritages. *"Thank you, Your Highness."*

"Call me Willa."

The image of the petite blonde female next to the large blond male flashed in her mind. Arie smiled. *"I need to get to work. When will your men be here?"*

After she heard the timeframe, she figured she could get the information needed, or pretend she had, and get the females out safely. Her fingers flew across the keyboard. Modern technology, one of the things she loved most about this century. The file with Laikyn O'Neil's information popped up, but when she opened it, nothing was inside. Arie google searched the female, and found she was a doctor, and was a partner with the Cordells. Her stomach churned in jealousy. She pushed her own feelings aside and tried to find out more about the elusive female.

An inner alarm had her looking up at the cameras to the outside of the building. Arie recognized the stretch limo as that of Nigel. She didn't want to face him just yet. Wondering why he was back so soon, she made quick work of getting all the info of Laikyn on a file for him, showing she'd tried, then flashed to the apartment where three feeders were lounging. Their gasps were cut off as she swept them into her arms and flashed them from the building. Nigel would have felt the power surge, but since she'd never used any around him before, she hoped he would not recognize it as hers. Three more bounces, and she deposited each female in their homes, making sure their minds were wiped.

By the time she was done, Arie needed to feed, but the thought of feeding from a human made her nauseous. In that moment she truly hated being part vampire. Her last flash was to her own home, one Nigel had no clue about. Bagged blood wasn't nearly as good as that from the living, but Arie still refused to give in to the urge. It took three pints before she no longer wobbled on her three-inch stilettos.

"The only person I will feed from will be my mate," she swore.

Dawn was fast approaching, but she wasn't limited to the rise and fall of the sun like Nigel. Her boss would most likely be searching for her, which made her nervous. No matter what the Council thought, he was a very dangerous vampire. She'd seen what he could and would do when crossed. A shiver stole up her spine. The first time Nigel had shown what he did to someone he felt betrayed him had been fast and brutal. Well, fast in the master had acted swiftly. However, the beings had suffered. Arie gagged as she thought of that night.

They'd gone out to eat with clients to celebrate, Nigel procuring more property, something he seemed obsessed with. A man, who she'd recognized as another one of their kind, came up to their table. He'd spoken in a foreign language that Arie and their client didn't understand, but from the red flush that covered Nigel's face, he wasn't pleased with whatever was said. Soon after, Nigel excused them. Arie was sure the car would take her home, but Nigel instructed the driver to take them downtown to the old buildings that were used during Halloween for haunted houses.

"Come with me, Arie. You shall see what I do to those who challenge my rule." Nigel held his hand out to her.

The gravel parking lot was deserted, save for their limo and one other car with blacked out windows. Arie took Nigel's hand, feeling as if she'd just touched the devil himself.

Two doors on the other car opened. The male from the restaurant got out, followed by another. Each were smirking. "Nigel, maybe we should leave," she whispered.

His grip on her tightened. "Trust me."

They entered the abandoned building. Her heels echoing all around the space. Her impulse to reach out to the Council almost too great to ignore.

"Gentlemen. This is my assistant. She will make sure your families are made aware of your passing." Nigel boasted in a condescending tone.

"It is you who she will be mourning, little man. After I fuck her senseless."

Dear lord. What had she gotten herself into?

With precision, Nigel struck the first male who spoke, ripping his heart out without moving a muscle. One moment he was standing next to her, the next he had a still beating heart in his palm. "You were saying?" Nigel asked, then sank his fangs into the organ.

Arie covered her mouth with her hands.

"You will pay for that." The other male lunged for Nigel. Their bodies moving like lightening.

Arie jumped backward, making herself appear as small as possible against the old brick wall. She ignored the fact she was dressed in a pale pink Chanel dress suit. Or the fact it was one of her favorites and cost a mint. If she made it out of the old warehouse, she'd kiss the ground and thank the lord she was alive.

When she opened her eyes again, Nigel stood with the spine of the last male dangling from his hand. Blood coated him from head to toe, glee shimmered in his black eyes. She'd never feared the vamp until that very moment. Her heart lurched.

"You have no reason to fear me, young Arie. This male and his friend should have known better than to come into my space and challenge me. Now, word will spread, and others will not make the same mistake."

Arie wondered how others would know but didn't question him. He was crazed on blood lust.

He seemed to be waiting for an answer from her. Arie could only nod.

"Now, let us go. I abhor having to do this sort of thing."

Shaking the memory away, she went into her bedroom. The need for a shower overwhelming.

Chapter Seven

Kellen waited for Rowan and Lyric to leave. The need to erase the fear from Laikyn and make her his, made him and his wolf uneasy. Yes, as alpha he could find her, but as her mate they'd have a connection like none other.

"Are you okay," he asked Laikyn. Having another being take over your mind had to feel weird on a level he had no idea about.

She nodded. "I'm tired and feel like I need a shower."

They'd brought in her bags she'd packed that contained most of her clothes, putting them in the master bedroom. The masculine space was in need of a feminine touch, but he'd wanted his mate to be the one to make those changes. "Come on then. Let's get you settled."

If she wasn't up to making love with him, he'd be fine holding her all night. His wolf snorted.

Laikyn looked at his hand, then at him. "What? Not gonna pick me up and carry me off to your mancave?"

He walked over, invading her space. "Oh, I'll carry you off, anywhere and everywhere, Mon Chaton. I just thought you might want to walk this time."

"What I want is you to be you, and me to be me. That means don't pussy foot around, and I won't act like a simpering little girl, unless that's how we're playing at the time."

Damn! He swore his mouth went dry at the image of Laikyn dressed up as a schoolgirl, while he was fucking her from behind. Deviant? Yes. But he made no apologies. They were grown adults who made their own rules.

"What does your gorgeous mind want right now?" Kellen placed his hands on the granite counter on either side of Laikyn, caging her in.

Laikyn licked her lips. "First, I want you and me to shower, then I want you to have your wicked way with me. I want to give you control of my body.

You know that is what I want. You knew it years ago, Kellen."

He did. Kellen had found her in a human run BDSM club being lashed by a man who thought he knew how to wield a whip. The memory still had the power to make him want to rip the human's arms from his body and beat him with them. The only thing that had kept Kellen from following through with it was Laikyn murmuring his name. She'd glanced at him with her sparkling green eyes, a plea for him to take what she was offering, more than he could handle.

"If you hadn't already taken too many lashes that night, I'd have whipped your pretty little ass." He lifted her into his arms.

She nodded. "I was a really bad girl," she agreed.

And he was a dumbass for not tying her to him that night. He'd been too hammered and thought she was too young, too high on endorphins to know she was his. He wanted her to experience life before settling down with him. Kellen knew he wasn't an easy male to be with. He'd demand her attention, her submission to him on many levels. Something he wasn't sure she'd be willing to give at the time. His wolf had growled as he'd left her sleeping in the hotel the next day.

"Lake, you know that once I make you mine there will be no going back. We can talk about boundaries, but there are going to be limits that I will push. Are you ready for all that being mine means?" He asked while he carried her to his room, soon to be their room if she agreed.

Her head tilted. "Kellen, I was yours then. Yours to do with as you chose. Of course, in your dumb male brain, you chose to run."

She yelped when he slapped her ass. "First rule, you don't call your alpha names except God, Master, Sir, or my given name. You call me disparaging ones, and you will be punished."

Heat lit her eyes. "I'll be sure to remember that."

"Make sure you do, unless you like your ass to be on fire." He ran his hand over the spot he just hit.

Bypassing his California King bed, he walked into the large bathroom. Setting Laikyn on her feet, she rubbed against his front, every delicious curve igniting him. "Strip those clothes off unless you want me to do it for you. I'm not sure they'll still be wearable after I'm done though." Kellen dragged his T-shirt over his own head, unsnapping his jeans as he kicked off one boot then the other.

"Goddess, you are gorgeous." Laikyn's eyes widened.

Kellen bent and removed his socks, standing he was naked while she was still fully clothed. "You haven't taken a stitch of clothing off yet, female." He crossed his arms over his chest.

She quickly shimmied out of her clothes, making his mouth water. He still remembered her taste. Like the finest whiskey he'd ever drank.

"You're growling," she said, her arms hanging loosely at her sides.

He moved closer, opening the door behind her, and adjusting the water temperature. "You make me and my wolf crazy."

"I like that. My wolf is all preening in my head."

Kellen pictured Laikyn on all fours presenting her delectable ass to him. "Let's get you cleaned then we'll see about getting you preening." Her sweet arousal perfumed the air.

When she didn't move, he picked her up by the waist, loving how his hands didn't look too big for her. Mother Nature created this one being just for him.

"Dang it. I forgot to unpack my bath gel and stuff," Laikyn muttered.

"That's okay. You're just gonna smell like me anyway." He placed her under the warm spray, then began lathering up his hands with his body wash. If he had his way, she'd always smell like him, from her head to her toes.

"I can see what you are thinking, Mr. Styles." She leaned into his touch, her breasts filling his palms.

"Good," he grunted. Bullshit. It was perfect. He brushed his body against hers, igniting all the nerve endings on his body. He measured her breasts in his palms, weighing them as he cupped them, rubbing his thumbs back and forth across the nipples. The slight hitch in her breathing let him know she liked what he was doing.

He turned her around, facing the cold tile wall of the shower, his front pressed against her back. Using his thigh, he split her legs apart. She shuddered against the bunched muscles of his leg.

"Oh, God, more." Laikyn reached back for his dick, but he grabbed her wrists and placed them on the wall.

"Not yet." Lathering up his hands with shampoo, he washed her hair then ran his fingers down her back, rubbing her shoulders and along her sides till he reached the rounded curve of her ass. "Damn, I love your ass." He ran his finger between the crack, when she tensed up, he gave a firm tap to one cheek. "This is mine. Right, Mon Chaton?"

"Yes!" She glanced over her shoulder, drops of water falling over them.

Kellen grabbed the shower head. "Close your eyes, baby." He waited till she turned back to face the wall, knowing she'd listen to him. He rinsed her hair, then replaced the shower head before lathering up his hands with more shower gel. Kneeling, he washed Laikyn's legs from her feet up, pausing at the apex of her thighs. She pushed her ass back at him, needing him to touch her there, but he ignored her silent command.

"My turn," he said, lifting Laikyn away from the wall and taking her place under the spray.

"Hey, what about me," she pouted up at him.

He raised one brow. "I cleaned you. Quite thoroughly I might add." He held the bodywash out to Laikyn. His cock bobbing in front of them, the heavy length too hard to stay upright.

"Um, is that thing bigger than before?" She asked.

"He'll fit," he promised. In all honesty he was a little worried himself. His dick appeared larger than ever.

"Fine, but if you split me in two, I'm the only doctor around here." She wagged a soapy finger at him.

Kellen laughed, then groaned as her hands began stroking his chest. Torture. Sweet torture was what she was doing to him.

Laikyn knelt in front of him, doing the same as he did to her, washing every inch of him except the part begging for her lips. Finally, she grasped him, the thick stalk of his cock barely fit in her grip.

His eyes nearly slid to the back of his head as her hand slid up his cock, her slick palm moving easily with the soap. With her on the floor, kneeling at his feet, Kellen was sure he'd never seen a more beautiful sight. The large mushroom shaped head of his dick was purple and almost painful to the touch with its need for release. Kellen wanted their first time, the time he claimed her to be on their bed. Not in the shower. He pulled her hand off him, making her squeak as he lifted her. "Not here."

He stepped from the shower, shutting the water off before drawing her with him. Using a large fluffy towel, Kellen made quick work of getting the water off them both, then lifted her into his arms and swept her into the bedroom. His large bed was a work of art. The big black wooden frame was solid, with the post thicker than his legs.

"Tonight, I make you mine." Kellen kissed Laikyn, their lips meeting, molding like their bodies.

She threaded her hands in his hair, holding him to her. "And I make you mine."

He let out a sound, a cross between a growl and a groan. Laikyn was done with the teasing, the tormenting. She wanted to get on with the claiming.

Kellen sat her on the waist high bed. She might have protested the loss of contact but being able to watch the flex and play of his naked ass, while he lit a few candles, gave her a moment to catch her breath. He picked up a remote, and immediately the stone fireplace roared to life, creating an ambiance all in itself. The green-eyed monster reared its ugly head.

Kellen spun back to face her, an alarmed look on his too handsome face. He closed the distance between them, coming back to her side and pressed her onto her back. The soft bedding cushioning her back. "What were you thinking?" He leaned down, resuming his exploration of her body with kisses.

She turned her head to face the dancing flames.

"Look at me, Mon Chaton."

"I just wondered how many other women you've set up the scene for like this." She waved her hand in the air.

A sharp nip of his teeth on the top of her breast had her gasping.

"I've not brought other women here, Lake. This was... is my home. The place I meant for me, my mate, and our children someday. I didn't want it smelling like another female."

Had she thought he'd lie, or somehow had a parade of women in and out of this room, she'd still have wanted him. Now, knowing she was the first, the banked need in her rose, flaring to life with more intensity than she'd thought possible. "I love you, Kellen."

Others may expect the male to say they loved them first, but she was not like others. Uncertainty was in the glowing blue eyes of the male she loved.

The teasing male was gone, replaced by the alpha ready to claim his mate. Laikyn was more than ready herself. She gripped him by the back of his head, pulling him down for a deep searing kiss, biting his lower lip. The small taste of him set her wolf at ease.

"Ah, my Chaton has claws I see." He chuckled against her lips, his own teeth gripped her tongue and nipped, not enough to draw blood.

Kellen wedged his legs between hers, then shook his head. "Not like this."

His words didn't make sense, until she found herself lifted, and placed in the middle, the comforter tossed to the bottom.

The head of his cock brushed the entrance to her pussy. She wondered if he was just going to plunge inside, but the tip brushed the lips of her sex, then retreated. His lips claimed hers, fierce and hungry. Words escaped her as he threaded their hands together above their heads.

Oh, my gawd. She'd never felt so cherished as she did, having Kellen cover every inch of her skin with his.

She dug her nails into the backs of his hands, then he was releasing her. "Keep your hands there, or I'll be forced to restrain you." Wicked intent was stamped on his features.

Her back arched at his slow exploration of her body. First, he began by kissing the column of her throat, followed by a small bite that drew a little blood. Not enough for a marking. Then he was moving down her body with small nips and licks, torturing her with his teeth and tongue. Laikyn wasn't sure who was making the mewling sounds, until Kellen growled from between her thighs.

"Fuck me, you are so damn wet." He swiped his tongue through her slit. "So damn good. I could make a meal of you." Another swipe of his tongue and then he buried his face where she needed him, eating her like he'd promised. Not missing one sensitive inch. With one hand he held her open, while the other he used to enter her with one broad finger, followed by another.

Laikyn was sure she was stretched to the max when a third finger was added next to the first two.

His head lifted. "That's it, baby. Ride my fingers."

Her hips rotated against his face, grinding herself against him for all she was worth, and she gave no fucks. It was fucking awesome. He mastered her body.

Her mouth opened to tell him she was close. That she needed more, but Kellen knew her body. "Come for me, Mon Chaton," he growled against her clit, then he sucked the hardened nub into his mouth, pumping the digits inside her in the same rhythm he sucked.

On a soundless scream, she came, arching her back. Her arms above her head wanted to come down and push him away, or hold him to her, she wasn't sure. The pleasure... intensity almost too much rolling through her.

"You come so beautifully. Next time you will scream my name," Kellen assured her.

The feel of him pushing inside, the stretch almost too much. Yet she knew the pleasure would only get better once he was seated inside her. Laikyn breathed deeply, trying to relax enough to allow him entry. His slow penetration a testament to his strength. Inch by slow glorious inch he moved back and forth until they were pressed groin to groin.

"See, perfect fit." He grinned down at her.

"I need to touch you." She tilted her head backward.

Kellen bent and kissed her. "I want you to touch me, too. Fuck! I need you to." He gripped her right thigh, opening her up further for him. "Hold on tight, baby."

She thought he murmured don't ever let me go, but his hips pulled back and powered back in. Laikyn lost all thought except the feel of Kellen. Sweat coated their bodies. She loved the play of Kellen's muscles as he strained above her. With each forward and backward motion, she swore he pushed her closer to the edge of oblivion.

"So close, Kellen." Her head thrashed on the red sheets.

He snatched her nape in one palm, forcing her gaze to his. "You're my mate. Say it, Laikyn," he growled.

A groan was his answer, but she knew he needed the words as much as she did. "Yours. I'm yours."

He withdrew, then slammed home again. Sensation climbed from her toes to the tips of her ears. Too much. Not enough.

As if he knew exactly what she needed, his hand went between them, pressing and pinching her clit. Just as the climax hit, she turned her neck to the side exposing her throat for him.

A bellow from his beast or him, she wasn't sure, came from Kellen. Then, he yelled, "Mine!" Sinking his canines into her skin, thrusting his cock deeply as come exploded from him.

"Kellen, I'm... Oh, God! I'm coming again!" She wasn't sure how long she rocked on his length, milking him for all she was worth. Pinpoints of light flashed behind her closed eyes, and she wished that his seed would indeed create a child within her.

His cock pulsed, jet after jet of come filling her.

Still buried within her, Kellen raised his head. "Never has that ever happened."

Laikyn enjoyed the feel of Kellen licking the wound on her neck, then his words penetrated. "What do you mean?"

The feel of his dick jerking inside her made her body clench down on him. "That. If I was a betting man, I'd say we could've just made a baby tonight, love."

Tears stung her eyes. "Oh. Would you be upset?"

He pulled back and thrust forward. "Baby, I am so far from upset. When you're ready, I'm ready to make a baby with you. I need you to mark me still."

Her gums ached to do just that. With him still inside her, he rolled them. "I love your tattoos." She ran her hand over the intricate details up one arm and down the other.

"You can explore to your heart's content later." He gripped her by the hips, moving her up and down. "Ride me, sweetheart."

Dear heaven, looking at him, and his rock-hard abs covered in tattoos, or his biceps so large she was sure he could lift a truck... made her pussy clench around his dick.

Kellen hissed in a breath. "Whatever the hell you are thinking keep it up. Fuck, you're squeezing my dick like a vice." His big hands clamped down on her waist, holding her still. "Mark me when you come, baby."

At the thought, Laikyn shuddered. Cool air brushed her nipples, making her gasp. She was glad he was doing the moving of the lower bodies, as she lost all of her senses. She leaned down and licked the tendon opposite of where he'd bitten her, enjoying the texture of his skin. Both arms were covered in tattoos, but he'd left one spot open, the place she was claiming as hers. Her canines dropped, and she scraped them back and forth.

Kellen pulled her hair, forcing her to his neck. "I can't wait to feel your teeth in me. Do it, now."

The imagery, his words, and the movement of their bodies made her wetter, had her clenching on him.

"Yeah, you like that, too. Make me yours." He gave a sharp tug.

With a cry, Laikyn bit down, piercing the skin and drinking in his essence. Like a blast their link snapped together. She came in a rush, sealing the wound as she cried out his name.

He flipped them again, pistoning his hips in a wild beat. The tightening around his cock became a pinpoint of pleasure until she was sure she'd pass out from it.

Their hearts began to beat in the same rhythm. She stared up at him, wondering if he noticed. He nodded, a smile playing on his lips, then his head descended, and he gripped her shoulder where he'd marked her. And then she was soaring into another climax. Hot and sweet, and relentless all balled together. She didn't realize she'd bitten him at the same time, and released him to scream, "Kellen, love you so much!"

"Fucking love, you, too." Kellen pounded into her unmercifully, racing toward his own orgasm. With a hoarse shout, he held her hips still as he surged into her again and again. His seed shot out, filling her with more of his come.

Laikyn stared up at her mate, happiness filling her at the words he'd muttered. She could only hope he'd repeat them when they weren't in the throes of passion.

Lying next to Kellen, she waited for him to comment. He stroked her back, the sweat cooling on both their bodies. She'd not had another lover and wasn't sure what to expect.

"Come on. You should take a bath while I make us a sandwich."

Those words were not what she'd expected. However, he'd come so much cleaning up a bit would make her rest more comfortably. Although she'd gladly sleep with the reminder of him inside her. Her stomach chose that moment to let out an unladylike growl.

"I can cook for us." She braced her chin on his chest.

"Of course, you can," he agreed.

He pressed a kiss to her nose. "However, I'll do the fixing, while you take a hot bath. You're gonna be sore, and I want you rested." Kellen inhaled.

There were no take backs when two wolves mated. So why was she so nervous he was about to do just that?

"Laikyn, I'm not sorry for mating you. I'm only sorry I waited so long, so whatever has you strung up tighter than a coil needs to stop."

She didn't know how to explain what she was feeling. Hell, she wasn't sure why she was so insecure. Instead, she nodded.

Kellen slid out of the bed, pulling her into his arms.

"Go take a bath, and when I'm done with whipping something together, I'll come get you." He patted her ass, giving her a slight shove toward the open doorway.

"I'll hurry," she assured him.

Chapter Eight

Kellen waited until he heard the water running before heading to the spare room for a quick shower. After he finished, he strolled toward the kitchen, the sounds of Laikyn in the master suite almost had him spinning on his feet and joining her. His empty stomach made him continue on. He'd just told a female... his mate that he loved her. His heart didn't stop, nor did his brain scream at him to run for the hills. In all actuality, he truly did love Laikyn. Never did he expect to fall for his mate, especially not so soon. Scratch that, he realized he'd been falling for her for years. The fact he'd let her run from him for two fucking years was his fault. His wolf growled in agreement.

Looking through the fridge he found the fixings for BLTs and macaroni and cheese he knew was in the cabinet. Not a gourmet meal by any stretch of the imagination, but something he wouldn't burn. Once he set the pot on the stove with enough water in it for the noodles, he got to work on frying up the bacon and slicing the tomatoes. He had the bread toasted, lettuce perfectly piled next to the tomatoes, and the macaroni warming when Laikyn came out in a pair of shorts and tank top.

He wondered if she realized she'd been the first female he'd fucked since the last time he'd been with her. Since finding her all but being fucked in a club she shouldn't have been in without him, his wolf, along with his junk wouldn't rise for any other female. Now, she waltzes in wearing a not too sexy outfit, and he was ready to rip the pieces of fabric off. The sound of her rumbling stomach put his needs at bay.

"Have a seat. What would you like to eat?" Damn! Now, he was sounding like Barney Fucking Homemaker.

She blinked. "Alright. What have you done with my alpha?"

Completely unafraid of tugging a wolf's tail, Laikyn invaded his space. Her clean scent wafting up to him. "I've no clue, but you better take advantage of his absence, little girl."

"Hmm, I think I will. The bacon smells amazing." She reached around and snagged a piece.

Watching her chew, the perfectly fried piece of pork was a sensual experience in itself. A bit of crumb landed on her lower lip. Before she could swipe it up with her tongue, Kellen's head bent, his mouth taking her lower lip into his, sucking it inside his, loving the hint of Laikyn and the tangy taste of bacon mixed together.

"You taste better. Come on, I better feed you before I devour you," he teased.

Kellen had to set her away from him or he'd jerk her poor excuse for shorts down and fuck her where they stood. The sweats he'd thrown on did nothing to hide the erection he was sporting, and the little minx knew it.

Her gaze went down to the bulge, then back up to his face. "That looks painful."

"Your ass is gonna be painful if you don't go sit down." He turned her toward the built-in seating area off the kitchen. The red leather circular benches were large enough to seat at least eight people.

Kellen placed the platters in the middle of the table, along with a pitcher of sweet tea, knowing that Laikyn loved the stuff. He grabbed a bottle of beer for himself, then sat across from his mate.

"Thank you for this." She waved at the food.

"My pleasure. Now dig in, so I can take you back to bed for a few hours of sleep. I need to rest a little before heading to the club tonight."

They ate in companionable silence. Kellen polished off most of the bacon and macaroni and cheese, then Laikyn stood. "You cooked so I clean, and don't argue."

He sat back with a satisfied groan. "No arguments from me. Have at it."

She worked efficiently around his kitchen, while he enjoyed watching her bend over and place the dishes in the dishwasher. He was such an ass man, and not afraid to admit it. And Laikyn had the finest one he'd seen. As she turned to him, uncertainty on her gorgeous face, he stood.

"Come. It's time to go back to bed. I haven't held you through the night."

She looked at the rising sun.

"You know what I mean. Don't sass me, mate." Kellen lifted her, tossing a giggling Laikyn over his shoulder. "Now, I'm going to have to punish you." He gave her a mock slap on her firm behind.

"Oh, whatever shall I do?"

He loved that she felt at ease enough to tease him. Flat out, he loved her. However, they needed to set some ground rules… at some point. Right now, he had to bury himself inside his very own piece of heaven.

Walking into the bedroom, he was surprised to see she'd changed the sheets and remade the bed. "You've been busy," he remarked, pulling the cover back.

Laikyn wiggled around until he let her slide down to the ground. "The sheets needed to be replaced after our... you know?" Scarlet stained her cheeks.

Kellen tipped her chin up to meet his eyes. "After I fucked you senseless and came in you so hard my eyes crossed?"

She licked her lips, making him groan.

"You are such a dirty talker."

"Baby, you ain't heard nothing yet. Wanna know what I want to do to you?" He rubbed his thumb across her bottom lip, rubbing the wetness into his skin. He wanted to have her scent all over him.

"I'm pretty sure you'd shock me senseless with your dirty mind." Arousal spiked the air. His and hers.

"I'm gonna ask you the same question I asked before. Do you like those clothes, cause I'm gonna rip them from your body in two point two seconds if you don't get them off? Actually, there is a house rule. From this second on, you wear no clothes once you enter this room." Kellen stared hard at Laikyn, wanting her to know he was serious. He didn't want any barrier between her body and him. He'd allow her to wear clothing outside of their bedroom, but once inside, she was to be bare. His for the taking.

"You're serious, aren't you?" Her voice trembled, but she lifted the hem of her top over her head.

He'd known she was braless in the kitchen, but seeing the hardened tips made his mouth water. He stepped back and waited for her to take off the shorts, watching her hook her thumbs in the elastic waistband. Laikyn did a little shimmy, and then the pale-yellow briefs fell to the floor. His cock jerked inside the nylon sweats at the image of his own personal goddess standing before him, gloriously naked.

"Now, undress me," his voice came out a rough growl.

Laikyn blinked, then raised her hands, inching the pants down and over his dick. "My, what is that?" she whispered sweetly.

Kellen stood with his legs locked as she pulled the fabric all the way to his ankles, kneeling as he lifted one foot then the other. His ability to speak had left him it seemed.

"May I?" She asked, palming his dick.

Holy shit. He wanted to shove his length between her parted lips but decided to see what she would do. Her mouth opened, taking the tip inside and sucked. Hard. Laikyn hummed. The sound had him going up on his toes.

"Fuck me, Lake. Feels so damn good." He gripped the hair on the back of her head. His control kept him from forcing her to take more, when that was exactly what he wanted—her to take all of him.

She teased the sensitive underside with her tongue, cupping his balls with one hand and held him in the other. If he didn't know better, he'd think she'd done this a thousand times. When her tongue began swirling down his length while she took as much of him as she could, the ability to think was lost to him. He felt his come bubbling up.

Breathless. She scraped her nails down his thigh, her lips and tongue stroking down his shaft threatened to make him explode. He could feel his cock flexing inside her tight mouth. The scent of her own arousal spiked the air around them.

"That's it, baby, right there," he groaned as she squeezed his balls and her mouth tightened on the head of his dick. "Fuck, you are getting wet, aren't you? Damn! I want to taste your pussy while you suck me."

His words had more of her sweet scent filling the room.

Her hand began stroking him from root to tip, just below her mouth as she sucked the engorged head of his erection.

Another hum had him close to coming, erotic pleasure singed him.

Why had he let her go two years ago? She was his everything.

Her caressing fingers tightened on his balls as she lashed at the underside of his dick with her tongue, humming a tune only she heard.

He tried to pull her off, his fingers tightened on the hair in his fist. Shards of pleasure arced up his spine. She shook her head and sucked harder, taking him deeper, swallowing against the tip. The pressure too much. He flexed his hips, shifting, and thrust against her face.

"Ah, Mon Chaton. So good. Too much," he swore. "Hell, if you don't want me coming down your throat you better stop now."

Her lips tightened. Her tongue lashing faster, moving faster on his flesh and he became lost to the pleasure she gave him.

Kellen found himself fucking her face, shuttling in and out in abandon, stroking over her tongue as he came. "Ah shit, Lake." He pushed to the back and held her head in place. "Take it," he growled, dominance in his tone. "Don't spill a drop."

Laikyn worked her mouth over his cock, her tongue licking, taking everything, he had and damn if he didn't love every second of it.

He didn't think he'd ever come so hard in his life. The feel of her throat tightening around the tip of his cock, the feel of her tongue lashing him, pushed him over the edge. Now, looking at the satisfied face of his mate, he knew he had to show her who was in charge.

Moments passed before he pulled out and then he lifted Laikyn from her knees. "On the bed, baby. Spread your knees, arms above your head."

She brushed the mass of red hair from her face but did as he said. Laying in the middle of his bed, her face flushed with excitement. Her folds slick with her juices. The sight made him hungry to taste, made him want to shove his dick in and fuck. Instead, he walked around the side and before she knew what he was about to do, he rifled through her things and found a pair of stockings in one of her bags. Using one set, he tied her left arm to the post at the top. "You ready to play, sweets?"

Nodding, her eyes looked hungry. He was one lucky wolf.

He walked around the bed, running the silky length of the remaining stocking through his fingers.

"What if I get scared?" She asked.

"You want a safe word?" He grabbed her other arm, tying it to the right post.

"Yes. I think so. Shouldn't I have one?"

His little kitten. He climbed between her thighs. Happy she hadn't disobeyed him and pulled them together. "You will always be safe with me. I would never hurt you. Whenever your scent changes, I will know when you are no longer with me. However, you want a safe word, pick one."

He watched her chew on that full lower lip. "Platypus."

Nodding, he ran his palms down her smooth thighs. "Alright. If you call out that word, we'll stop and discuss what's going on. However, I will push your boundaries. We done talking now?"

She grinned and wiggled her ass. "Yes, Sir, Alpha Sir."

"That is three for your impertinence." Knowing he'd left enough play in the length, Kellen maneuvered her onto her belly, giving her three quick swats. Each one on a different area of her ass.

She yelped but he flipped her around. "You ready to behave?"

"Yes," she whispered, but her sweet arousal increased.

Kellen licked his lips, dying to taste the sweet elixir that was Laikyn.

He shifted down, wiggling until he had her thighs farther apart, the reddened bud of her clit begging for attention. "Good girl. You know what good girls get?" He looked up. "They get to come." Kellen needed to feel her orgasm explode on his tongue and then around his dick one more time before they slept.

Laikyn couldn't believe how much pleasure she'd gotten from sucking Kellen. Nor could she control the cry he elicited as he swiped his tongue through her folds. She was certain the male was going to torture her with long, slow licks. She was on edge, primed and ready to explode, needing him to send her soaring sooner, rather than later.

Wicked, laughing eyes such a bright blue they glowed up at her. A grin tugged at his lips. The sight had her tummy flipping, heart racing in anticipation.

His lips surrounded her clit, sucking it into his mouth, and his tongue lashed it, playing with it. With one hand lying on her stomach, his teeth joined the torment, searing pleasure-pain for only a moment before he suckled at it with firm, sweet draws.

She was certain flames would take her away on a wave of heat as he repeated each suck, nip, lick, and hungry kiss to her sensitive nub. Laikyn struggled against the restraints, trying to touch him.

Kellen raised his head. "You want me to stop?"

Slick with perspiration, she shook her head. Finally satisfied she would obey, he lowered his head again, capturing her clit between his teeth, a wicked light in his eyes. Two thick fingers entered at the same time his lips drew on the hardened bud, drawing on it tighter. The erotic feeling went straight to her core, arcing her body making her explode into an orgasm fast and furious.

With her thighs spread, knees bent, arms restrained, she was completely at his mercy. Kellen did nothing by half measures, working her over, taking his time, he devoured everything she had, licking her folds as his fingers eased out of her.

One broad digit smoothed down, pressing against her rear entrance. "I'm going to take you here. Not now, but soon."

She tensed at his words. Her head lifted, watching him stare back at her. His long tongue peeked out, working over her. She didn't think she could come again, but Kellen proved to be a master at manipulating a female's body. Using the juices from her body he continued to tease the entrance to her ass, sucking her clit at the same time. By the time she was begging for him to make her come he'd pushed his finger deep, past the ring of muscles, creating a whole new need in her.

Laikyn fell back, unable to watch while the pleasure sent her spiraling toward another pinnacle.

Her hips arched, and another finger joined the first in her ass, fucking her with bold thrusts she'd never thought to enjoy. His mouth and tongue working her pussy, sucked, flicked, and bit the swollen bud, sending explosions of ecstasy from her head to her toes. Muscles tightening, a kaleidoscope of colors flashed behind her eyelids throwing her into another release. "Goddess, yes, Kellen."

She shuddered, every nerve in her body tightened, her body jerked with aftershocks. Her pussy clenched in need.

"Kellen, please," she begged.

"My name on your lips when you come is like music to my ears." Kellen's voice was a deep rough growl. "I love the way you beg. Your pussy and ass are so tight. It's like heaven when I sink into you."

He moved over her, the head of his cock pressed inside, and then eased out.

Laikyn didn't think she could come again. The in and out friction of Kellen's dick, shuttling back and forth as he buried himself as deeply as he could get, pressing down on her clit with each downward thrust had her screaming his name.

Her wrists being released, and then the feel of his hands rubbing over the muscles of her shoulders barely registered before his hands moved to her hips.

"I want to feel you coming around me again, Mon Chaton." Kellen was driving in and out of her with the force of a supernova. "Move with me, baby. That's it," he groaned in her ear.

Lifting up into his thrusts, she couldn't stop herself from arching, trying to keep up with his fast thrusts. His pistoning strokes ignited a flame in her that built, searing her with a pleasure, driving her to another orgasm that shocked them both when she came.

Kellen called out her name when he came in a strangled and tight voice. His release throbbed inside her, and then he bit down on the spot he'd marked her, making them both jerk and come again. The feeling seeming to never end, burning through her and through their combined link, she felt his emotions, the rapture lashing back and forth, until he collapsed on top of her.

Completely boneless, and exhausted, Laikyn lay under him unable to move.

"I love you, Kellen," she murmured, licking the wound she made.

"Love you, too," he whispered. "So fucking much, it scares me. I'd rip the world apart for you."

And she knew he did and would thanks to their link. Having the connection snap into place there was nothing they could hide from each other. A scary thing, but she was glad. Except now she couldn't think bad things about him.

"You are still due for a few more punishments for past infractions." Kellen lifted up on his forearms.

Laikyn hooked her arms around his neck. "If your punishment includes lots of big Os, I'm totally game." She ruined the announcement with a yawn.

Her mate shook his head, then rolled out of bed. "Stay right there," he ordered.

She wanted to salute but wasn't up to another round of his form of *punishment* just yet.

"I heard that." Kellen came back in with a wet cloth in one hand and a dry one over his shoulder.

Laikyn had taken care of patients, had the male between her legs on an up close and personal level minutes ago. But, having him wipe a damp washcloth, cleaning her up, then dry her, made heat crawl up her face. Damn her red-haired genetics.

Laughing, he tossed the cloths in through the open door to the bathroom. "You're cute when you blush." The bed dipped as he climbed in. "Let's get a couple hours rest." He pulled the blanket over them.

With a nod, she rolled into him, feeling his big arm hold her tight to his chest, she fell asleep almost immediately.

Chapter Nine

Kellen hated leaving Laikyn, but the needs of the pack called. He walked into the club, glancing around at the dozens of faces staring back at him. Heads bowed in respect as he strolled past. A few murmured words of respect, others nodded.

He shook his head and walked to the raised dais that usually held the DJ. Xan stood there, his mate next to him, making Kellen's lips twitch. "Your balls get lost?" Kellen asked.

Xan raised his middle finger, pulling Breezy closer to his side, kissing her full on the lips in front of the crowd.

"Yeah, I see that you have."

"Alright, settle down everyone," Kellen yelled loud enough he didn't need the microphone to be heard. "I've got some shit to say, and I don't want to repeat myself. I called this meeting and for those who are not here, I will be sending this out through the pack link. However, I had hoped all available would make it." He glanced around, making eye contact with each member he saw. The Iron Wolves consisted of more than just a biker club. They had doctors, lawyers, nurses, teachers, businessmen and women. The club was where they could come and let loose, be themselves without fear of the human world finding out about them. The apartments attached to the back had been built years ago, going far below the ground, creating a sanctuary away from the prying eyes of humans in case of an emergency. There, they could safely live and hide, if the need arose.

Now, he wondered if the underground world would be more of a danger than a sanctuary with this new threat. Taking a deep breath, he explained what they'd found in Kansas City, then told them of the threat on the road near his home. Gasps and cries of outrage filled the large room.

He let them vent for a minute or so, then raised his fist. When the murmurs continued, he let his wolf come forward, a growl rent the air. Instant obedience settled around him.

"Like I was trying to explain. We are now aware and can prepare. I want each of you to be on guard. Nobody is to go out alone until this threat is eliminated. Period. I don't want any of you to leave with anyone you don't personally know, and if you have any doubts, then call for help. I'd rather have a bunch of false calls, than the alternative. Feel me?" He let them assimilate his words before continuing. "Now, it's time for the fun part. I could tell you what to look for, but in order for you to truly know, I'm going to show you. It's gonna be a mindfuck of epic proportions. The twin vamps who helped me are okay for bloodsuckers, but I want you to trust your gut as well." He breathed out heavily.

"I'll add my strength to you, Alpha." Xan breathed out steadily.

Kellen nodded in his direction. "Here we go boys and girls. I'd lie and say this ain't gonna hurt, but it might." He let the silence settle, then he opened his mind to the pack. Long moments passed, emotions clogged the room, thickening the air. Eyes filled with fear, but he continued until he was sure they all had the knowledge needed.

"The Cordells? They seem honorable?" Xan spoke low.

"Yeah, but sometimes honor can be forgotten when a male wants something badly enough. I think they realized what they wanted, wasn't really theirs to begin with, and are cool. I'd rip their fucking throats out and shit down their necks if they tried to take what's mine," Kellen promised him.

Rueful amusement filled Xan's gaze. "Nice description."

"And on that note, I got to get to work." Breezy interrupted them.

"You gonna let him have his balls back before you leave." Kellen quirked a brow.

Breezy patted Xan's dick. "His balls are perfectly fine where they are. Oh, and I'll let Laikyn know what you said. I'm sure she'll find it hilarious, too." She smiled sweetly. "Not." She danced away before Kellen could stop her.

"What the hell is she talking about?" He pointed at the blonde with pink and purple hair his second thought the sun rose and set on.

Xan stared after his mate. "I think Laikyn is going to be stopping in at the hospital or some shit. Fuck if I know."

"Bullshit." Kellen jumped from the dais, already opening his link to Laikyn in his mind.

"Laikyn, what the hell is this shit about you going to the hospital today?" His tone was more wolf than man.

"Hello to you too, Kellen. Remember, I am a doctor? Doctors need to work. Hospitals are where doctors usually do that." He pictured her rolling her green eyes while she finger combed her hair.

"That is five, baby. Now, let's start again. Why didn't you tell me you had plans to go to the hospital today?" There, he sounded a little more human.

Laikyn breathed loudly, a sure sign she was trying to stay calm, a sound he heard like a deep gust of air. *"We didn't do a whole lot of talking, and then you were already gone when I got up. I'd always planned on going to the hospital today. I have a meeting with the board about a position there. It's a formality really."*

Kellen didn't stop to talk to anyone as he left the club, raising his head he inhaled before he hopped into his rig. *"I'm coming to get you. Consider me your glorified chauffeur."*

"Kellen, seriously, that's crazy. I could be hours. Don't you have a pack to manage?"

He could give zero fucks about anyone or anything except keeping his mate safe. Instead of telling her that, he floored it to his home. *"I'll be there shortly. What time do you need to be at the hospital?"* When he heard the time, disappointment hit him that they wouldn't have time for a little afternoon delight. Her husky laugh let him know she caught his thoughts.

"I promise to make it up to you. I better go so I can finish getting ready. Love you," Laikyn said.

Even through the link he enjoyed hearing her say the words. *"Right back atcha,"* he assured her.

Using all his senses like Damien and Luke had shown him was getting easier. When he pulled into his garage, he made sure the wards were set and secure. His cell buzzed, making him pause in his steps. Looking at the caller ID, he didn't recognize the number.

"Styles here," he growled.

"Hello, Kellen. My name is Niall. I'm the alpha of the Mystic Wolves. I believe we have a lot to discuss."

Kellen gripped the phone in his hand. The deep baritone let him know the male was indeed an alpha in his own right. "Is Taya alright?"

"She will be. Although she's been through a lot, our healers have assured me she will be fine in time."

He nodded. The female had been kidnapped and brutalized by a rival pack a few months back. A young female held and at the mercy of men, wolves who had no honor, sometimes chose death over living with the memory of what they'd been through. Taya was stronger than anyone had given her credit. She and Xan had been casual, but he was sure the female wanted more, until Xan found his mate in Breezy. Kellen shook his head; glad she'd found a new home with the Mystic Wolves.

"That's not why I'm calling you." Niall's voice cut through his musings.

The ominous words made him stop in his tracks. "Spit it the fuck out, man."

Niall laughed. "I knew I'd like you. Alright, here it is. Our Fey have seen some strange shit and said you would need some added protection."

Kellen took the phone away from his ear, looked at it then brought it back. "Did you say Fey? Like little beings with pointy ears and wings?" Damn! His world was getting all kinds of messed up.

"Dude, you've been watching Lord of the Rings too much." Niall spoke to someone in the background. "My mate said she'd love a pair of fairy wings, too. Anyway, no, the Fey don't have those. You are probably freaking a bit, and I don't blame you. The truth is, if we exist, then why is it hard to imagine there are other beings? Of course, I too had no idea there were vampires. I thought they were truly mythical. You know, movies and books only creatures. So, back to the message I was to give you. You are going to need the help of a Fey, and not another vamp in order to beat this one."

"Awesome. Where do I find this Fey?" His eyes lit on his mate walking in wearing a pair of pale-yellow capri pants and a white top that fit snuggly to her breasts. The button-down shirt drew his gaze, making him want to use his teeth rip it open.

"We have someone who wants to come and help, if you are willing."

"How will I know this person is not a danger to us?" He held his hand out to Laikyn, needing to feel her in his arms.

A heavy sigh interrupted his musings. "Kellen, as one alpha to the other, you know we could open a link and share information. Do you want to do that?"

Without having met the other man, he wasn't willing to do that. "You come here, and I'll agree. Over the phone, that would be no."

"That's what I thought. Trust me. When you see the Fey, you'll know it's safe. Well, you'll know they are not there to harm you or your pack. Believe me when I say they are much better friends than enemies, and right now, we need more friends than enemies," Niall growled.

"When will this Fey be here, and are they male or female?"

"Her name is Jennaveve. Tiny blonde creature. You can't miss her. She is like a drill sergeant and will try to boss you around. I'd say not to let her, but yeah, good luck with that."

Feminine laughter in the background had his eyes narrowing. "Is she old or young? You're being very vague, asshole."

"Hi, Kellen. May I call you, Kellen, or do you prefer Mr. Styles?"

Laikyn stiffened at his side. "Is this Niall's mate, Alaina?" Kellen asked, pulling his mate closer.

"Oh, good. You've heard of me. All good things I presume?" She paused, then continued. "Anyhoo, what my mate is trying and failing to say is this. Jennaveve is a feisty little thing who is a born leader. We don't know her age, and don't even ask. She gets this tick in her right eye and things rattle all around. Creepy is what I call it. I'm part fey and part wolf, but I still hide behind Niall when she gets *that* look. My point is, she is awesome as long as you don't piss her off. So, don't piss her off. Hey, I was just trying to be helpful." Alaina's words trailed off.

"Sorry about that. My lovely mate… is wonderful," Niall said, his words sounded pained.

Kellen looked into Laikyn's eyes. "You would be over my knee in an instant."

"Promises promises." She stood on her tiptoes and kissed his chin.

"TMI, man." Niall's words stopped him from tossing the phone down.

"Fine. So, I watch for a tiny blonde who I will want to throttle. Gotcha."

"When Jenna gets there, if you have any questions, or you want to verify her credentials, give me a holler. Talk to you soon," Niall said.

Pocketing the device, he shook his head. "Damn it, I should have asked when she was coming and what to expect."

Laikyn patted his chest. "You did, remember. I believe you were warned not to ask."

He growled as his mate's hands traveled over his chest. "You sure you need to head to the hospital?" His dick twitched at the need to bury itself inside the welcoming body nestling up to him.

"Most definitely need to. However, I will totally make it up to you," she promised.

Images of her on all fours while he prepared her ass to take him flashed in his mind. "We should go before I make you late for your meeting."

Laikyn licked her lips. That flush he was coming to love crept up her neck.

His wolf whined.

Kellen jerked her closer, covering her slick mouth with his, devouring her like the animal he was. The taste of strawberry lip gloss fueled his hunger as he fed on her, licking along the seams, demanding entry. His hands gripped her ass, bringing her body against his. Laikyn's gasp gave him access to the inside of her mouth. Taking complete advantage, his left hand moved up her back to the slim column of her neck, holding her in place while he fed off of her. Tongues sliding against each other, dueling, he growled and sucked hers into his mouth.

The clock over the garage door chimed. It took all his control to break away from the all-consuming kiss. He pressed his forehead against hers. "Damn, baby. You make me lose my head."

Breath coming in pants Laikyn didn't answer.

"Let's go." Kellen ran his hand through the hair he'd messed up.

"Let me grab my bag," Laikyn said.

The drive to the hospital was one of endurance on her part, when all she wanted to do was tell her mate to pull over. The idea of him taking her, dominating her in any place turned her on.

"I can smell your need, Mon Chaton." His fingers tapped the wheel with one hand, while the other reached for hers.

Laughing, she looked over at him. "Of course, you can. You're the big bad alpha."

He sighed. "Mate, have you no fear of all the punishments you are racking up?"

She ran her thumb over the rings he wore on his hand. "I trust you to never truly hurt me. Besides, the idea of your hands on me, makes me wet."

"Fuck! You can't say shit like that while I'm driving," he swore swerving as a deer ran out in front of them.

The ring with four claws raking down it in titanium was a work of art. The large piece of jewelry was worn on his middle finger. All the men wore similar ones, but Kellen and Xan's were the largest, and her mate had two blue stones between the claws like eyes. The same as his second-in-command. Laikyn thought of getting one commissioned for herself, only instead of blue stones, she'd get emerald like her eyes.

"I'll make it so." Kellen read her mind, flipping their hands, and rubbing his thumb over her fingers.

"Oh, gawd. Is that presumptuous of me?"

Kellen pulled her hand onto his lap, placing it over the large erection. "The idea of you wearing more of me, in any way, makes me fucking hard."

She laughed. "Everything makes you hard."

He shook his head. "That is where you're wrong. For two god damn years, the only thing that made me get a woody, were thoughts of you."

His admission had her heart accelerating. Could it be true? Kellen Styles, the biggest player of the Iron Wolves. The most sought-after wolf for miles around. The male who could truly have any female who walked into the club hadn't slept with another female since he'd taken her virginity. Her wolf scented no lies. She pictured the red girl shaking her tail and preening like a damn idiot.

"Well, I only got a wetty with visions of you, so we are even." Her voice hitched as his cock jerked beneath her palm.

"Oh, I'll have you shaking your tail alright." Kellen pressed her hand a little firmer between his legs. "Only you won't be a little red wolf, you'll be a female and I'll have you more than preening, baby."

There was not a doubt in her mind he could and would do just that. Hell, she was ready to do just that right then and there. The sight of the hospital had her pulling her hand away, making Kellen groan.

"You can just drop me off in the front—" Laikyn didn't continue her words when Kellen ignored her, driving into the visitors parking garage.

He glanced over at Laikyn. "I'll just hang out in the lobby outside the area your interview or whatever is taking place."

The tone of his voice said there was no use in arguing. "How do I look?" she asked when he opened her door and helped her down.

"Good enough to eat," he replied, eyes scanning the area.

Laikyn thought he was taking the whole protecting his mate thing a little too seriously, but she held her tongue.

She had her favorite designer bag with its C logo strapped over her chest and her briefcase in her hand with all her credentials in case they asked for them. Although she didn't think they'd need them since all her info had been either emailed or faxed. Her palms became damp the closer she got to the head of the surgery unit. Having been a partner in the practice back in Kansas City, Laikyn hadn't answered to anyone except the Cordells, and they were often times too laid back. Now that she knew more about them, she understood they were far older and wiser than all who ran the hospitals today.

"You'll be fine. Besides, if you don't want to work, you know I can support you and about ten others without blinking, right?" His words interrupted her musings.

Yeah, she was aware Kellen was very wealthy, not only from the club and the custom work they did on cars and trucks, but his family had been around for a long time, too.

"I know. But I love what I do." She took a deep breath.

He held the door open to the suite where she'd told him her interview was. The receptionist looked up, doing a double take at Kellen who gave her a nod and then took a seat.

Laikyn ignored the fact the young female was clearly checking out her mate. "I have an appointment with Dr. Niffen."

After her name was verified, Laikyn sat down beside Kellen. Within moments, the door opened, and a distinguished older female appeared. "Dr. O'Neil?"

Standing, she gave Kellen's hand a squeeze then walked up to the door. "Dr. Niffen?"

"Yes. I'm so pleased you agreed to meet with me. Please come back to my office."

The gleam of anticipation in the girl's eyes behind the reception desk had Laikyn reaching out to Kellen. *"You have an admirer."*

"The only one I'm interested in, is a sexy redhead with an ass made for my palms, and a pussy made for my dick, not to mention other places on her body. When we get home, I plan to take advantage of a few of those. You best focus on your interview, instead of me fucking you till we're both too tired to do anything else. Besides, I don't want this chick to think my hard-on is because of her," Kellen growled.

She saw him flash an image of him lifting one booted foot up to rest on his jean clad knee. Then he pulled his phone out and began scrolling through what she assumed were his emails. The male was truly awesome on so many levels.

"Please, have a seat."

Laikyn blinked, not realizing she'd walked like a zombie into the spacious office of the head of surgery. Holy crap! She'd thought the twins' office was opulent, but this one took it to a whole new level.

"Thank you for seeing me. I wasn't sure there would be an opening so close to my home." Laikyn worked to keep her voice even.

Dr. Niffen folded her hands on top of her desk. "You'll be an asset to this hospital, Dr. O'Neil, not to mention you come highly recommended. I'm prepared to offer you a position now if you are amiable."

A packet was pushed toward her. Laikyn wondered who had been the one to *highly recommend* her, but the figure staring up at her was more than she'd expected. "Wow, this is an amazing sum." Laikyn tapped the paper. "When do I start?" She didn't try to keep the excitement out of her voice.

"Don't you want to take the time to look over all the documents inside and have your lawyer look over them?" Dr. Niffen sat back with a slight smile.

Laikyn opened her senses, inhaling deeply. She smelled no subterfuge, only the scent of one hundred percent human, and a feline that Laikyn was sure was a calico cat. A normal house cat at that.

"Fine. I'll read over them really quick. I'm a fast reader." True to her word, she flipped through each page, carefully reading each word. Everything seemed in order, she didn't get any bad feelings like she'd gotten before.

"Where do I sign?" She held her hand out.

Dr. Niffen laughed. "You're a very smart young lady. Once you sign, I'll sign, and we'll begin the process. Actually, it's pretty quick since we've already begun."

She scrawled her signature on several pieces of paper, filled out the tax documents, and sat back with a happy sigh. "I can't wait to begin working here."

The phone rang, interrupting her. Dr. Niffen held up her hand. Laikyn couldn't help but hear the other end of the conversation, and when the receiver was replaced, she was prepared for the meeting to end.

"I apologize, but I have a patient that I need to see. If you were already on staff, I'd take you with me. Next time," Dr. Niffen assured.

Laikyn and Dr. Niffen stood at the same time, walking back the way they'd come. She took the time to look at the other offices they passed. The ones with the open doors were almost as nice as Dr. Niffen's.

"We'll see you in a few days, Dr. O'Neil. Lila, be a dear and send these down to Human Resources."

Lila stood. The brunette was almost as tall as Laikyn. "Absolutely. Welcome to the team, Dr. O'Neil."

"Thank you. Lila?" Laikyn held her hand out.

The cool fingers were firm as they gripped hers. "Yes. Lila Grant."

"It's nice to meet you." Laikyn could sense the woman had looked at Kellen, but hadn't tried to poach, which moved her up a notch.

"You'll love it here. All the doctors in the practice are very pleasant to work for, and I love our patients." Sincerity rang in her tone.

Yeah, she'd made a great choice.

"I can't wait to get started. Have a great day, Lila." Turning to Dr. Niffen, Laikyn held her hand out. "Whenever you have a firm date, just give me a call. My schedule is open."

"We'll see you in a couple days. Until then, enjoy your time off." Dr. Niffen looked over to where Kellen unfolded himself from a lounge chair.

He walked forward with his usual confident swagger. "This is my—" she trailed off, not wanting to say mate.

"Hello, my name is Kellen. I'm Laikyn's fiancé. It's very nice to meet you. Her car is in the shop, and I had some things to get done in town. I thought we'd kill two birds with one stone." He held his hand out to the doctor, and Laikyn swore the woman looked ready to swoon.

Introductions were made, and in typical Kellen style, he had the older woman eating out of the palm of his hand. Tattooed badass men clearly didn't faze Dr. Niffen.

"We'll be on our way so you can get to your meeting. It was a pleasure meeting you, Joy." Kellen kissed her boss's cheek. The fact the other woman had told him to call her by her first name had made Lila raise her eyebrows. Obviously not something that was done on the daily.

In the elevator she waited until the doors closed before turning to him. "You realize you are a menace to all women?"

He crossed his arms over his chest, a smirk on his face. "How you figure?"

"Joy? She told you to call her Joy after two minutes." She couldn't help but smile.

Kellen unfolded his arms, reaching for Laikyn. "The only female I care about is you. I'm glad she felt comfortable with me. Sometimes I can scare people."

She snorted. "Sometimes?"

He nuzzled her neck. "Only when the need arises."

"Hmm, I think there is a whole other need arising now." She pushed her pelvis in close to his. The ping of the elevator had her stilling in his embrace. "I better watch myself when I'm in my place of work," she said pulling away before the doors swooshed open.

"For now, I'll let you." The words had a thrill shooting through her.

Several people piled in, keeping her from voicing anything out loud. A little girl tugged on her mother's hand, bringing the harried female's attention to her. Laikyn and Kellen could hear her whispered words as she asked why her daddy was so sick, and if he was going to survive. The mother picked the little girl up and cuddled her close. Laikyn met the somber brown eyed gaze of the child over her mother's shoulder. Clutched in her tiny fist was a stuffed wolf with sparkling blue eyes.

"I like your stuffed animal," Laikyn murmured to the little girl.

"My daddy gave it to me. He said wolves were the fiercest of all and they protected their own." She sniffed, dropping the toy.

Laikyn bent, the scent that hit her was that of a shifter. Wolf to be exact. She pretended to drop her purse, knowing Kellen would help her out. With so many bodies in the elevator, she and Kellen hadn't thought, or at least she hadn't thought to scent their surroundings. Kellen's blue eyes narrowed on the toy in her hand, then glanced at the woman and child.

"Sorry, I dropped my purse getting this." She stood after making sure Kellen had inhaled the scents on the stuffed wolf.

"Thank you," the young mom murmured.

On the ground floor the duo headed toward the cafeteria. "I don't recognize the scent, but he's at least part wolf. I smelled human, but that could be the mother. Shit!" Kellen ran his hand over his head, looking around. "You are gonna ask me to try, aren't you?"

"If he's a shifter, or part but never shifted, whatever is wrong with him—" she stopped herself.

As a doctor she wanted to fix everyone. Not knowing anything about the male whose child smelled like wolf, made both the female, and shifter in Laikyn want to fix them.

"Mon Chaton, it's not that easy. If he's in bad shape, the wolf's bite could kill him. Or..." he held up his hand stalling her. "The shifter we smelled on the toy could very well be the mother, and not him." Kellen said too low for anyone but her to hear.

Her brain was aware what he said was a possibility, but in her heart, she couldn't squash the part of her that needed to find out, one way or the other.

Kellen growled. "You're set on finding out more. Aren't you?"

Her head moved up and down.

"Fine, but we do this my way, or I will toss you over my shoulder, and I don't give a flying fuck what it looks like. Feel me?"

"I fucking love you."

The blue of his eyes flashed to that of his wolf. "Damn, you are so making up for this. I hope you don't have any plans after this, cause the only ones are going to be me, you, my cock, and your pussy. Whatever I decide, wherever I decide, I will take you. I'm not asking, baby. Just letting you know."

The air around them thickened. Without a doubt he could smell how his words turned her on, but Laikyn thought, in Kellen's words, she gave no fucks. After they tracked down the little girl and mama, and found out a little more, she was surrendering her body to that of her mate. Her alpha.

Dang it, she hated walking around with wet panties.

Kellen's husky laugh had her reaching for his hand.

Chapter Ten

Laikyn scanned the cafeteria, looking for two people in the large crowd was almost impossible. How were they to find their query amongst all the humans, especially one little girl with ponytails and her mother. A sense of loss threatened to bring her to tears, until Kellen tapped her nose.

"Take a deep breath," he instructed.

Near the doors leading to the outside courtyard was the little girl and her mom. Their heads were bent close together with two trays of food in front of them.

"Should we get some food and go sit with them?" Nervousness made her palms sweat.

Kellen's body heat soothed her. "No. Let's get this over with. Just go over and introduce yourself. I'll stand back so I don't scare them."

Her eyes darted up to the male beside her. "You're going to let me go over there alone?"

His husky laugh had several people turning toward them. "Not on your life, baby. I'll be real close, just not too close. Come on." He steered her around a couple.

The closer they got, the heavier the scent of shifter became. Laikyn squeezed Kellen's fingers, hoping he'd understand.

"*The child is part wolf.*" He spoke through their link.

Her own sense of smell wasn't the same as his. More than likely him being the alpha gave him super sniffing ability as well. She sent him an image of Scooby Doo, getting a quick flash of her over his lap. "*Stop that, or everyone will smell me, human or not,*" she admonished.

"*Then don't compare me to a damn dog.*"

"*Woof,*" she joked, then stopped as they reached the table. In that moment the knowledge that Kellen had diverted her attention registered. She was one lucky gal indeed.

His hand slipped from hers as she took the remaining steps toward the pair. One pair of amber eyes blinked up at Laikyn with so much knowledge, she swore the little girl's wolf was letting her know she was there.

"Hi. My name is Dr. Laikyn O'Neil. May I speak with you?" She pulled her gaze from the child to the mother. Green eyes stared at her in alarm.

"Is my husband, okay? We just left him." She asked in a shaky voice.

"Oh, I'm sorry. I don't have news about your husband. I actually wanted to ask you some questions. May I sit down?" Laikyn smiled, hoping to ease them.

The mother waved at the chairs across from them.

"Mommy, she's like me and daddy," the little girl announced.

"What do you mean, Dakota?" Alarmed, the mother pulled the young girl onto her lap, staring at Laikyn like she'd grown two heads.

"I guess that answers one of our questions." Laikyn didn't look at Kellen as she spoke to him through their mate bond.

"Dakota. What a lovely name for a little girl." Laikyn focused on the human mother. "What's your name, miss?"

"Mommy, don't be scared. Her wolf is much stronger than mine, and mine is not scared."

The mother's hand trembled, making Laikyn's protective instincts kick in. "We are not here to harm you. I am new to the hospital and happened to smell shifter in the elevator. My mate and I followed you down here to find out more. Where is your," Laikyn looked to the child before continuing, "father?"

"Oh, god. What is going on? I thought he was the only one. We thought... I mean," she whispered roughly. "Jared and I met in college at NDSU. I always knew he was different, but not *that* different. His senses were sharper, and he could run, jump, and do things much better than most others. He could have gone on to the NFL, but we got pregnant with this little nugget, and as the saying goes. The rest was history." She took a ragged breath. "We were on vacation, hiking the Black Hills. It'll be fun, he said." She gave a hollow laugh. "There was a bear trap on a trail. We didn't see it until it was too late. I got on my cell phone right away. Within hours he was flown here, but he's not getting better. We don't understand." Tears streamed down her cheeks.

"What is your name," Kellen growled.

Dakota stared at Laikyn's mate, her eyes going wide. "Oh wow. You are even bigger than my daddy."

Kellen squatted down to eye level. "My name is Kellen Styles. I'm what you would call the alpha. Leader of the pack if you will. What is your name, ma'am?" His blue eyes turned toward Dakota's mother.

Laikyn watched the young woman squirm. "Irene Carpenter, and this is our daughter Dakota. Do you know what is wrong with Jared? Can you help us since you're the alpha or whatever?"

He shrugged massive shoulders. "Take me to him, and I'll see what's going on. I make no promises, but between myself, Laikyn and my pack, there's a chance."

Irene stood with Dakota in her arms. "Let's go."

Her mate shook his head. "After you."

"Mommy, my wolf is squirming. I think we're supposed to listen to him." Dakota's voice cut through the tension.

"Sweetheart, if they fix your daddy, I'll bow down, curtsy or whatever you say. Right now, I want your daddy fixed." Irene kissed Dakota's forehead, then hefted her up higher on her hip.

"Here, let me take her," Kellen reached for Dakota.

Irene's mouth opened, but the little girl practically leaped into Kellen's arms.

Laikyn shook her head. "He has a way with the female population. Of course, I will only allow the ones under the age of maybe eight or nine to get away with that." Laikyn pointed her thumb at

Dakota, who was now sitting on Kellen's shoulders, and laughed as she joined Irene in her fast clip toward the bank of elevators.

"He is a handsome devil. My Jared is, too. Although he is the opposite of your... mate. Are you two not married?" Irene pressed the button for the fifth floor, her hesitation on the words made Laikyn aware of the fact the woman, and Jared were either completely unaware of his heritage, or the wolf was running. From what or who, was yet to be known.

"We call ourselves mates, but I will expect him to put a ring on it too. A huge one. He will be getting his tattooed on, so all the women know he is taken." Laikyn looked over her shoulder, meeting the heat in her mate's blue eyes.

"Mon Chaton, you can have anything you want. I'll have your name tattooed around anything you desire." He winked.

Goddess, she loved his dirty mind.

The doors opened to their floor, and then they didn't need Irene to tell them where Jared was. The

scent of a shifter in pain hit Laikyn hard. As a doctor she picked up the pace, leaving Irene behind along with Kellen and Dakota. The door to the room was closed, but she pushed it open without thinking.

A snarl greeted her from the bed. The large male sat up, a feral look in his eye. "Who are you?"

Kellen pushed past her, a growl rumbling out. "That is my mate, boy."

Laikyn's hand found the fisted one of Kellen's. "He's in so much pain."

"I can see that." Never taking his eyes off of Jared, Kellen walked closer. "I know what you are, and you obviously know what we are. What you don't know is that we are friends and are here to help."

"Daddy, these are my friends. My wolf is at ease around them. Well, not at first around Alpha, but now it is," Dakota said, trying to break free from her mother. "Mommy, let me go. I told you, it's okay. They are gonna fix daddy." Her little voice wobbled.

Jared held his hand out to his family. "Come here," he growled.

"My name is Dr. Laikyn O'Neil. Let me look at your injury." She gestured at the foot of the bed.

All the strength seemed to evaporate from the male in the bed.

"Jared, let them see. What can it hurt?" Irene lifted the blanket, showing Laikyn and Kellen.

Her training kept the gasp from escaping. *"Why or who would have silver traps laid out along hiking trails?"*

"Fuck if I know. Hell, I don't think any shifter goes on hikes where humans are." Kellen bent closer.

"When did this happen?" Kellen asked Jared.

"Two days ago." His arm dropped from around Irene.

The angry red and swollen leg had blood red veins sticking out. A clear sign of infection and blood poisoning.

"Jared, were you a born shifter, or turned?" Kellen asked.

Laikyn watched the two males. Trepidation had her nerves on edge. If a wolf was out turning others, and not taking care of them, the shifter community in itself could be in trouble.

"I was born this way I believe. Now, if you want to know who my birth parents are or were, you're shit out of luck. I grew up with wonderful parents, but they adopted a little boy they thought was human. It wasn't until I shifted that they realized their little guy was a freak of nature. By then they loved me in spite of my issues, so I suppressed the urge, and went on with my life." His speaking clearly wore him out. With his breathing becoming more labored, Laikyn feared they might be too late.

The door opened on a silent swoosh. Kellen turned, his eyes taking in the tiny blonde female wearing a lab coat. She smelled like honey and mint. Not human.

Moving quickly, he placed himself in front of Laikyn. "Who are you?" Authority rang in his voice.

With a wave of her hand, the small female walked forward. "And a hello to you too, Kellen Styles of the Iron Wolves. I've come to save the day, and not a moment too soon, I see." She tsked a few times, setting Kellen on edge.

"Hi, my name is Laikyn. Can I help you?" She tried to look around Kellen.

"Oh, down little wolfey. I don't want your mate. Or yours, young lady. He reeks of infection."

Kellen growled, his wolf wanting to shake her. "Female, who the fuck are you?"

She held her hand up. "Boy, I do believe you need your mouth washed out. There is a child in this room." She smiled pleasantly and gave a tiny finger wave at Dakota. "Well, aren't you just the cutest little thing. Yes, you are. Oh yes you are."

"Enough. Who are you?" Kellen allowed his alpha powers to flare.

Sighing, she tilted her head. "I am Jennaveve Grey from Mystic. Your aura led me to you. You really need to learn to hide yourself a little better, Alpha. Now, down boy. This one needs my attention, and then we will go see about your other problem."

Kellen couldn't believe the little Fey female was completely unfazed by his anger. Her body and scent didn't show one iota of sense, or fear.

"I really like her," Laikyn whispered.

He grunted. "You would."

They stared in awe while Jennaveve ran her hand over the elevated leg, a slight glow from her hands went into the wound, then flowed up through the veins. Within minutes Jared's fevered eyes opened, no longer glassy.

"Son of a bitch. I feel like I just got tackled," he groaned.

Irene let out a hiccupping cry. "How do you feel?"

The angry redness was almost completely gone.

"Other than weak, I no longer fear I'm leaving my two best girls." Jared met Kellen's eyes, then looked away. "You're like me." It was a statement.

Nodding, Kellen waited for the Fey to finish before he moved. Whatever she was doing to heal Jared was working.

"Alright, that'll do it. I left the outer injury for looks. You know, humans get all weirded out when something mysterious happens. Request to be let out and sign one of those against doc orders thingies. You'll be just fine in a day or so. Rest and relaxation are just what the Fey orders. I'm the Fey by the way." She clapped her hands, then dusted them on her black leggings.

"Mommy, where are her wings?" Irene put her hand over Dakota's mouth.

Jennaveve raised her hands. "That is what I asked. I mean, seriously. I should have sparkly wings and fairy dust. But nope. Didn't get them." She shrugged her shoulders, turning back to Kellen and Laikyn. "You ready to blow this popcorn stand or what?"

"I need to speak with Jared. If you and Laikyn would like to wait by the door." He pointed toward the entrance, knowing his mate would understand his need to get pertinent info from the family.

"Man, if you are going to threaten me and mine, I'll tell you right now you're barking up the wrong tree," Jared growled, his eyes trying to stay focused.

Kellen instantly liked the younger man. "No, I'm not. However, I would like to extend a bit of help and knowledge to you."

Jared shook his head. "I don't need it. I haven't shifted since I was a kid, and I don't plan to do it anytime soon." Finality rang out.

Although Kellen couldn't fathom not shifting, the amount of willpower it took to suppress your wolf had to be great. "If you change your mind and want to meet others of your kind, we are more than a pack. We're family. You, my friend, are family. Even if you don't acknowledge it." Kellen nodded at Dakota.

"Thank you for the offer." Jared held his hand out to Irene.

Grabbing his wallet out of his back pocket, Kellen pulled out his card with the Iron Wolves logo on it. He looked around for a pen, then smiled as Laikyn placed one from her bag in his hand. "Thank you," he said, giving her a quick kiss. Quickly, he added his cell to the card.

"This is the number to the shop and my cell. If you need anything, or want to find out more, give me a call. If I'm not available ask for Xan. He's my second."

Jared took the card, looking at the four claws raking down the front and the stylized wording, then back at Kellen. "Thank you for coming and being cool to my family. Jennaveve, thank you for saving my life."

The little Fey came back to the bed. "Aw, wolfman, you should stop suppressing your beast. He's not happy, and neither is the one inside your little one, or the little one inside your mate."

Irene gasped, her hand going to her tummy. "How did you know?"

Jennaveve smiled. "I know because I'm smart like that." Her laugh was infectious, but not to the trio that had stunned looks. Kellen understood.

"Like I said. If you change your mind, give me a holler. Dakota, it was nice meeting you and your mama. Take care of her and your daddy." He ruffled the blonde hair on top the little girl's head.

"You're a good man. Just like my daddy" She made a little woof sound that had the adults smiling.

Spinning, he grabbed Laikyn around the waist. "Let's get the hell out of here." His blue eyes sparkled.

"Really, Kellen, what is going on?" Laikyn asked as he pulled the door open, steering them out of the room.

"We need to leave." He wasn't ready to have kids saying he was a good man. Hell, he was so far from good.

Jennaveve followed behind them. "I call shotgun."

Kellen pinched the bridge of his nose. "How exactly did you get here?"

"Ancient secret. If I tell you. I'd have to—" She made a slicing motion across her throat, then giggled like a loon.

"You can ride with us, but you're in the backseat. No arguments."

The crazy thing saluted him, clicking her heels together like she was a soldier. "Yes,

Sir, Alpha Sir."

"I'm being punished, aren't I?" He looked into the green eyes of his mate, and wished they were alone.

"Just remember what happens to good boys." She pressed up against him.

"I'm right here, folks. No sex talk. It makes me all freaked out. You do not want a freaked-out Fey on your hands." She shuddered.

Kellen looked up.

"Whatcha looking for?" Jennaveve asked.

"Men in white coats to swoop in and take you away." He looked around as they waited for the elevator to arrive.

"Never fear. I am not crazy. Well, crazy is as crazy does. Isn't that how the saying goes?"

His mate burst out laughing. The tiny blonde who couldn't be more than five two or five feet three inches tall, looked totally serious.

"I have a saying and it goes something like," he paused for a second, "don't feed the crazy."

Laikyn looking horrified stared at the Fey who began laughing.

"I do believe we are going to get along famously. Yep, just like two pickles in a jar, you, and I." Jennaveve winked.

"I think you mean two peas in a pod," Laikyn corrected.

Jennaveve shook her head. "Nope. I don't really like peas. Those little green suckers are nasty. Now, pickles are delicious." She smacked her lips together.

Kellen decided to keep quiet

They made it back out to his vehicle without incident, with Jennaveve asking Laikyn a shitton of questions he zoned out. He'd been inside Jared's head and was able to extract his information even though some would say it was wrong. Being the alpha he had to put his pack first. An unknown shifter could be problematic for his kind. He wondered what the medical records said in regard to his blood work.

"Don't worry about that," Jennaveve said.

His hackles rose. "Get out of my head," he growled.

The little sprite shrugged. "Build better walls. I'll show you how to do that as well. You have a great start. As does your mate. But against what is to come, you'll need better. Where is this vehicle of yours?" She yawned.

He ground his teeth. "How exactly are you going to show my entire pack?"

With a wave she gave a smile. "I will tell you once you get me to your home. Now, I am tired. Do you know how much energy it takes to travel the way I did?"

Hell! She hadn't told him how she'd gotten there in the first place, so he didn't know shit, which pissed him the fuck off. A bit of knowledge she clearly knew.

"You alphas are all the same. It's so easy to tease you. Well would you look at that. Can I drive?" The Fey skipped to his XV.

Laikyn placed her palm on his arm. "I think she's adorable. Besides, we need all the help we can get."

His mind went back to the night the fog had surrounded them. "I see your point." And he did.

Like a gentleman, Kellen opened the backdoor for Jennaveve, a clear indication she was not driving his rig, nor was she riding up front. She patted his chest like she knew exactly what he was doing. A tinkling laugh floated out of the vehicle before he shut the door and looked up at the clear blue sky. He opened Laikyn's door, helping her in before striding around the front to get in himself, praying for patience.

"Such a gentlemen you are, Kellen Styles."

"Thank you. Would you like me to stop and grab you a bite to eat on the way back?"

"Nope. I'm going to rest my eyes. You may drive."

Again, she waved her hand, but he forced his jaw to relax, figuring he'd need his back teeth to tear into whatever animal he tracked down and killed in his wolf form.

Laikyn reached over the console, her small hand on his thigh had the muscles jumping. "I'll make sure you get a massage when we are alone."

"I just threw up in my mouth a little," Jennaveve muttered.

His battle to keep from grinding his molars was lost. It was going to be the longest couple of days, he was sure.

Chapter Eleven

Laikyn barely controlled her mirth at the Fey's constant goading of her mate. Kellen wasn't used to anyone teasing him. Well, she could get away with it, but only if they were naked, but then she would pay for it. Images of what he'd do to her had her squirming in the seat.

"That is one way to distract me from throttling the little thing in the back."

She kept her eyes straight ahead, concentrating on fortifying the walls between her and all except Kellen. *"I hope she can't see what I was showing you."*

"I thought you liked being a little exhibitionist." Kellen's blue eyes looked her way.

A slight snore interrupted them.

"The Fey are a mystery. Do you think she will share with us more about them?" Laikyn would love to know more, especially since she'd seen the

way the other female was able to heal Jared. Humans would have been able to survive from the injury, unless they were allergic to the silver the way a shifter was. Jared had no knowledge of his allergy and would have died. Stubborn male.

"Men don't like to feel vulnerable. I'm sure Jared will be more aware now."

She pictured the sweet face of the little girl. *"I hate the thought of them being all alone out there without pack."*

Her mate sent a smile that warmed her heart. *"I have a feeling we will see them again."*

The gates of the club appeared. Rowan's truck sat next to Syn's and several others along with a dozen motorcycles. *"Well, I guess we shall see how she reacts to our motley crew."* Laikyn kept her fingers entwined with Kellen's as he down shifted the gears.

Jennaveve sat up as if she'd not just been snoring. "Well, isn't this a nice establishment. You sure do like that symbol." Her head nodded at the claws on the side of the brick building.

"We are the Iron Wolves." Kellen backed into his spot.

"Silver is your kryptonite, so makes sense. You think whoever owns that truck will let me drive it?" She pointed at Syn's black beast.

Kellen smirked. "You'll have to talk to my sister."

She made a noncommittal noise, but her large turquoise eyes stared out the window. "Your vehicles are remarkable."

Laikyn looked at the details on each one of the member's cars. The club wasn't just an MC. They owned and operated one of the most sought-after custom detail businesses in the country, turning the ordinary, into extraordinary. They were known for taking a common vehicle and customizing it with more bells and whistles than the average person needed. She ran her hand over Kellen's dashboard.

"I see," Jennaveve said.

"Dang it. I didn't block that, did I?" Laikyn looked over her shoulder.

The Fey shrugged. "I'll show you how to do it without thinking. If I needed wheels like you, I'd totally hire you to fix me one. I'd want an orange one though."

Kellen raised his brows. "Why orange?"

She sighed. "It's so bright. Like the sun. I'd want to have some splashes of red and yellow." Jennaveve showed Laikyn and Kellen what she meant. The color almost too bright.

"Yikes. I'd need sunglasses." Laikyn rubbed her eyes.

Kellen shut off the vehicle, turning to face the back. "Alright. Let's go into my office. I'll call a meeting with my second and a few of my top men and their women. From the looks of it, they're already here."

Jennaveve didn't wait for him to open her door, before hopping down.

"I believe she's ready." Laikyn pressed a quick kiss to Kellen's lips. He grabbed the back of her head, turning the small gesture into something more.

"Alright, kiddos. Let's not make babies with our mouths."

Kellen pulled away, resting his forehead on hers. "Remind me I can't throttle her."

Laughing, Laikyn licked her lips. "I think she's awesome."

"You would."

He flung his door open, then came around to her side, lifting her down with ease. "Let's roll."

His eyes scanned the area even though it was daylight. At the entrance to the club, he opened the door and entered first, then held the door open for Laikyn and Jennaveve. The action one the Fey was clearly used to. All eyes turned to them as they entered.

She and Kellen held hands, but she could tell that wasn't what caused the hackles to rise on the wolves. Jennaveve walked with her back straight, meeting the eyes of every male and female in the place. Even though they were in human form, all were wolves.

"Xan, Bodhi, Rowan. In my office. And bring your mates." He looked at the room. "I want everyone to stick around, I'll be calling a meeting of the pack to discuss the latest development."

Silence met his announcement.

Laikyn saw Breezy grip Xan's hand while Lyric moved closer to Rowan. Syn moved away from the crowd, coming toward Kellen.

"Brother, if I could have a word before your meeting?"

"What's up, sis?"

"You called everyone into the meeting but me. So, am I just to stand around out here and twiddle my thumbs? I got shit to do, so I thought I'd let you know you could just open our link and you could let me know."

Laikyn saw the hurt Kellen's announcement had made. "Fuck, Syn, I meant for you to be part of the rollcall. Damn," he growled. "Don't make me grovel. Get your ass in my office."

"Well, then next time don't call out everyone except me. I don't have a fucking mate, jackhole." Syn stomped past Kellen.

"Don't. You know she's hurting right now," Laikyn pleaded with Kellen. The brother and sister had identical temperaments.

"That's the only reason I'm allowing her to get away with this shit."

Syn seethed inside. She had no plans of sticking around, watching Bodhi check his phone, or slink off to speak with whoever was on the other line. Overhearing him growling orders to another person, like they were important to him made her realize she was beating her heart against a stone wall. All the years she'd waited for him to realize they were mates was for nothing. All the time she'd thought he was waiting for her to grow up, had been futile she'd realized when he'd called another female baby in a gentle tone. The same one he'd used on her when she'd been a kid and had been hurt over something. No more. Syn was done being the sweet little girl he thought she was. Hell, she was so far from the sweet innocent thing they all thought she was, but she'd tried to be what he seemed to want in a mate. And it had been for nothing.

"Hello. You must be Karsyn Styles. You look like your brother, only beautiful, and I like your truck."

Blinking down at the petite blonde, Syn suppressed a growl. "Who the heck are you, female?"

Unable to scent anything, she waited.

"My name is Jennaveve, but you can call me Jenna. We are going to be good friends. I can feel it. Well, and see it, but I don't want to freak you out. People tend to give me looks." Jenna made air quotes around the last word.

Syn looked over her shoulder at Kellen and Laikyn as they entered his office. "Is she crazy?"

Kellen shook his head, then stopped. "Probably, but she's Fey."

Like that answered her question. "So, what is a Fey?" Syn directed her words at the newcomer.

"Ah, child, if I told you I'd have to kill you." She made a slashing motion with her finger across her throat, then laughed. The sound too sweet to have come from a crazy lady.

"Are we protecting her?" Syn walked around the self-proclaimed Fey.

The rest of the Iron Wolves top enforcers entered, settling onto the couches, with their mates on their laps. Syn chose one of the large recliners facing away from Bodhi. She crossed her legs in the short mini skirt, showing off her legs. The feel of Bodhi's eyes following the movement usually made her want to tease him, but she was done with him.

Jenna stood off to the side, next to Kellen.

"This is Jennaveve. She's a Fey and from the Mystic Pack." Kellen didn't look or sound too pleased.

"Hello boys and girls. Or should I say pups. As your esteemed leader has announced, I am Fey, and you are all in need of some assistance. That is where I come in. Now, I know you all think you don't need it, because you all are big bad wolfies and I'm this little sprite. However, I can assure you, you do. Now, do you have any questions before I begin?" She gazed at each member.

Syn felt power swell, and it wasn't her brother Kellen.

"Alright, since you are all ready, prepare yourselves. It's gonna be a doozy, but it'll be over before you know it. Kellen, I suggest you and your mate take a seat." Jenna pointed at the chair."

Kellen nodded and took his recliner, pulling Laikyn onto his lap.

Not knowing what she'd expected, her head jerked back against the soft leather. Information filtered in quicker than anything she'd ever received. As her mind processed, sweat coated her brow. Minutes, or hours, passed before she opened her eyes.

When the hum in her head eased, Syn looked around, seeing stunned expressions on everyone else's faces.

"You've faced vampires before?" Kellen questioned Jenna.

Jenna nodded. "They are not all bad. The majority are good. You just need to know their strengths and weaknesses."

The men didn't look as shaken as she and the other women did. It took monumental effort for her to stand. Even then her legs threatened to buckle. Bodhi was the first to shoot to his feet, his hands on her hips steadying her. "Easy, sweets."

She jerked out of his arms. "Thanks, but I'm fine."

"You will be." Jenna's dark eyes assessed her, making Syn think she could see straight through to her soul.

"If there's nothing else, I'm outta here."

"Don't forget to keep with the buddy system, sis." Kellen got to his feet.

Envy hit Syn as she looked around at the three women snuggled in their mate's arms. Having known, or thought she'd known her mate since

childhood, Syn was sure she'd be the first to be mated. "Got it."

Before anyone else could stop her, she left. The echo from the heels of her cowgirl boots, was the only sound as she walked across the office. The urge to take one last look rode her, but Syn had gotten really good at denying her own needs. Bodhi was a need and a want she would be forgetting. If she had to find a different man or wolf every night for the rest of her life, she'd bury him beneath the scents of others who wanted her.

"Hey, Syn. You look like you could use a drink."

Syn looked at one of Breezy's twin brothers. They were identical twins. Her heart skipped a beat. What would it be like to have two men who loved her? One of the two blond men with liquid brown eyes held a bottle out between his fingers.

"I believe that is just what I need," she agreed.

Although her body only seemed to come alive for the mohawk bad boy, she was going to teach it

to want someone else. Multiple someone's if it killed her.

"Brother, let me give you a piece of advice." Kellen stared at Bodhi. "You'd better get your head out of your ass, before my sister decides to find a more amiable wolf."

Bodhi raised his middle finger. "You don't know shit, man."

Kellen tilted his head to the side. "That's where you're wrong."

"Unless you need me, I'm out." Bodhi stood waiting.

Laikyn snuggled up to Kellen, watching the other male walk out the side door instead of back into the club.

"He is going to fuck up the best thing." Kellen's tone lowered to a whisper.

Jennaveve spun in a circle. "Alright, let's go break it to the rest of the gang," she sang in a singsong voice.

He was about to correct her words, then saw the laughter in her eyes. "Are you going to mind fuck them as well?"

"It's the most expedient way. Don't you think?" She led the way back out.

His mate squeezed his hand, soothing his inner beast. "Let's get this over with. How long are you going to be with us?"

"Already tired of me?" The Fey pushed out the door, loud music filtered in.

"Not in the least," Kellen muttered.

"Do you have a burning sensation below your waist, Alpha?" Jennaveve asked.

"What the flying fuck are you talking about?"

Laikyn placed her hand over her mouth.

"You know? Liar, liar, pants on fire." The Fey waved her hand toward his groin area.

"Can I eat her?" The pleading tone had his mate bent over laughing.

"I love her. Like in a totally friendly, want to be her bestie way." Laikyn had tears streaming down her cheeks.

He lifted her up. "You won't be laughing when I have you tied to my bed this evening." He promised his mate.

Her laughter died, replaced by another warmth. "That is so not fair. Now everyone here will smell my need for you."

Kellen licked her lips. "Good. Now, be a good girl and sit at the bar next to—" His words trailed off at the sight of his baby sister on top the bar, and the Mattice twins doing body shots off her abdomen. His growl made the room go quiet except for the music blaring from the speaker.

"Shaw, Parker, get your fucking paws and lips off my sister. Now," he roared.

Syn sat up, a scowl on her beautiful face. "Big bro, we are having fun."

"Now pups, if you value your dicks." Kellen's growl became that of his beast.

Shaw and Parker backed away, hands up.

"Sorry, Alpha. We didn't know she was off limits," Parker said, eyes down.

Laikyn put her body between his and the other wolves. "Kellen, your sister is a big girl. You need to calm down."

He looked into his mate's eyes. "Move it, Lake. You don't know shit." Kellen set Laikyn aside, his soul focus on the trio at the bar.

"Brother, be a dear and go play with your own toys. I am just having some fun. You know... that thing that everyone does." Syn swung her legs over the edge of the counter.

Taking a deep breath, Kellen had to remember the Mattice brothers were not bad men. Otherwise, he'd end up gutting them both. A concept his wolf found satisfying, but the male pushed back. "You don't want this. Them," he said pointing at the wolves with their heads bent, not meeting his gaze.

His sister on the other hand had no problem facing his wrath, hopping down from the bar. "You need to mind your own damn business. If I want to have some fun, and if it happens to be with two men, it's really none of your fucking business." She poked him in the chest.

Kellen caught her hand in his, leaning down so their noses met. "Don't make me become the alpha in front of everyone here, Syn. You don't want me to embarrass you more than you've already done."

He released the tiny hand in his palm, anger shooting out of the blue eyes so like his own, his heart contracted at the hurt reflected out at him. With a nod, she scooped up the designer bag she'd tossed on the floor between the two bar stools. "I'm out." Two words was all Syn muttered as she stormed toward the side door.

"Who is your buddy, Syn," Kellen asked.

Her middle finger of her right hand raised up high in the air was his answer, making him growl. His feet took a few steps toward the door when Lyric and Rowan moved in front of him.

"We'll follow her," Lyric promised.

"Don't let her get into any trouble. You know how she gets when she's in a mood." Kellen watched his sister disappear from his sight.

Rowan and Lyric were already following out the door. Kellen turned to find his mate, cursing when she was not right next to him. The little Fey raised dark brows. He wondered if her blonde hair was natural as he realized the brows were a few shades darker.

"Nope, they've always been that way," she said.

"Fuck, get out of my mind." He glared at Jennaveve.

She shrugged, clearly unconcerned at his anger. "Stop broadcasting."

"Have you seen my mate?" He lifted his head, opening all his senses in his search for Laikyn.

Jennaveve did a slow circle. "She was here just a minute ago. Well, until you were mean to her that is. Maybe she went to the bathroom?"

"What the hell? When was I mean to her?" He placed his fists on his hips to keep from reaching out and shaking the Fey.

"When you told her, she didn't know crap. That was rude and uncalled for. I distinctly remember she looked like someone had just kicked her in the nuts… well, she doesn't have those. But the analogy stands."

Kellen didn't have time to figure out the female or her riddles. "Has anyone seen Laikyn?" He yelled.

Everyone looked at him like he'd grown two heads. How the hell did his mate sneak away without anyone noticing?

He went to the door where Wyck was standing guard. The big male had his arms folded over his broad chest, a scowl on his face. "You looking for your mate?"

Nodding, Kellen waited.

"She slipped out the back door about seven minutes ago. I'm thinking you fucked up, brother. The scent of her hurt was overwhelming."

Wyck's accusation made him feel like an ass. "How did she leave?" Kellen wasn't going to explain or apologize to anyone but his mate.

"I don't know. I thought she was just coming out for air." Wyck stood taller, his head lifting into the air.

"You know there is a rule that nobody is to go off alone, and that is especially true for females. Why the hell would you think it was okay for her to be out alone?" Kellen shoved the larger male against the side of the building, his body partially shifting.

"I'm sorry, Alpha." Wyck's quick apology eased some of his anger.

Jennaveve walked around them. "She's in your office."

Kellen released his hold, dropping Wyck as quickly as he'd picked him up. "How do you know this?"

She shrugged. "I tapped into her mind. She decided to take a shower."

Pointing at the Fey. "Watch her."

"Of course. She isn't really crazy, right?" Wyck stared down at Jennaveve.

Not feeling like appeasing the other wolf, Kellen left the two-standing outside.

Chapter Twelve

As soon as he entered his office, her scent hit him hard. Anger, humiliation and hurt mixed together, offending his senses. He did that to his mate with his careless words, and Kellen didn't know how to fix it. If he could turn back time and take back what he'd said, he'd do it. However, he was a male who accepted his faults and didn't make excuses for them. He was a grown ass man, who owned his shit. If he fucked up, which he knew he did occasionally, he owned it, and was quick to make amends. The question now was, how did he make his mate forgive him?

The sound of the water had his body reacting. He did something he'd never done in all the years of running the Iron Wolves. He locked the door to the outer office, keeping anyone from entering. Of course, they were wolves and could break down the door if they chose.

Grabbing the black T-shirt by the bottom, he pulled it over his head, dropping it on the floor as he walked. His boots were kicked off without a care in his haste to reach Laikyn. The belt buckle and then his jeans were undone before he reached the closed door. He wondered if she'd locked him out the way he'd locked the other door, surprised when the knob turned in his palm. He had his pants and briefs removed by the time he entered the steamy room.

The glass enclosure was no barrier between him and his mate. She made a startled little gasp when he pulled the door open. "What are you doing in here?" She asked, green eyes moist from her silent tears.

"I'm sorry. Goddess, I'm sorry I fucking hurt you. I'm an asshole of the king of asses." Kellen pulled her away from the spraying water.

Laikyn pushed the wet hair out of her face. "Yes, you are," she agreed.

Kellen tracked the soap running down the front of her body, watching her nipples bead up before his eyes. "You're so beautiful."

"You're in the doghouse." She raked her nails over his chest.

"Woof," he barked. Happy to see her smile.

"You hurt me." Her smile disappeared.

He pulled her into his arms, forgetting the fact his body demanded relief. "I know, and for that I'm sorry. I never meant to do that. Sometimes I speak without thinking."

She nodded against him. "You're male. I think it's a flaw of all your kind." He felt her smile against him, but her scent was still tinged with the acrid smell of hurt.

"Let me make it up to you." He smoothed his hands in a circular motion down her back.

Laikyn snorted. "With sex?"

Kellen pulled back. "No, baby. If you don't want me to touch you I won't. It'll kill me, but I'll leave you to your shower, but I meant by showing you through actions. I will mess up, but I will always, no matter what, apologize if I'm wrong and make amends to those that I've wronged. If they choose to not accept my apology." Kellen shrugged. "That is on them. I can't fix stupid." He smiled as she pinched his side.

"I love you, even though you are sometimes an ass." She raised up to press a kiss to his lips.

Before she could say another word, he maneuvered them so her back pressed against the tile wall, his mouth covered the sassy one of hers. Her quick exhale was taken in by him, and then no other words were needed. Kellen let his palms roam her wet curves, the soap allowed his hands to slide over every inch of her body. Using his knee, he motioned for her to move her legs further apart, which she quickly complied to do.

"Sweetheart, you do know I'll only tolerate name calling for a short time, right?" He bent and bit into his mark on her shoulder, loving the uncontrollable shudder that wracked her frame.

"Then what happens?" Laikyn wrapped her arms around him.

Her breathless words had him ready to fuck and fuck hard. So not a dominate male thing to do.

Well, not one that was in charge. He put a little space between their bodies, his hands finding hers. "I think I need to remind you who's in control here." Kellen pulled her arms above her head. "You think you're in charge, little girl?" He asked as water rained down on their sides.

Laikyn shook her head.

"Words, Lake," he growled.

"No," she stuttered.

His inner beast wasn't sure he believed her. "Keep your arms above your head. If you move one inch that I don't tell you to do, I'll stop. If I stop, you'll be punished."

Her sweet perfume filled the small space. He licked his lips, but resisted the urge to drop to his knees, and taste how sweet she was. Instead, he grabbed the body wash off the shelf and poured a generous portion into his palm. After he rubbed his hands together, he started on her hands then shoulders, and working his way down her arms, being sure to clean every inch. Repeating the process with her chest, but skipping over the little buds of her nipples, even though he could see she really wanted him to touch her there.

Pouring more of the scented soap into his palm, he knelt in front of Laikyn and worked his hands over her stomach, and down her thighs. It nearly killed him to be so close to her pussy, and not lean in and lick. "Lift your foot," he ordered, placing her right foot on his thigh as he cleaned between each toe.

Laikyn giggled. "That tickles."

"Hmm, I'll have to keep that in mind." He tapped the other leg, indicating she allow him to do the same with the left foot. After he cleaned her front thoroughly, he looked up the expanse of his mate's body, making a spinning motion with his finger. "Turn around. I need to make sure your back is clean."

He expected her to argue but was pleasantly surprised when she inhaled and then shimmied around in the small space, presenting him with her perfect heart shaped ass. Damn, he loved Laikyn O'Neil's fine as fuck ass. "Pour some soap in my hand." His words sounded more growl than he'd planned, but his mate quickly upended the bottle in his palm.

Kellen worked his way from her feet to the apex between her thighs, tracing his fingers between the crevice of her ass.

She tensed, looking over her shoulder. "Kellen?"

"I'm not going to take you here." His finger brushed against her back hole. "Not now, but I will claim you in every way imaginable. Make no mistake, Mon Chaton, you will accept me everywhere."

"I know." Her easy acceptance had him rising to his feet.

She'd turned to face the tiles, her arms above her head. "Do you now?" He asked.

His cock so hard, he worried the poor thing was going to burst.

The little minx blinked back at him over her shoulder. "Well, I mean, unless of course you choose not to. Which would be a shame, since I've been preparing myself for just that occasion these last two years."

Red. He saw red. "What the ever-loving fuck do you mean, preparing yourself?" His fingers gripped her hair.

Green eyes sparkled. "Not by taking other men up the ass, but you know, there are other ways… to you know… practice."

Images of her working a dildo up her own ass had his cock jerking against her. "Are you saying you've fucked your own ass, Laikyn?"

She tried to break eye contact with him, but he gripped her chin. "Don't turn away from me."

"I ached for you, and knew it was something you'd like."

He took a deep breath, trying to rein himself in. "You are trying to kill me." His slid his hands around, cupping her breasts while he kissed his mating mark.

"That would not be in my favor." She rubbed her ass against his straining erection.

Kellen bent, allowing his dick to run back and forth between her legs. "Such a smart female."

"You going to torment me all night, or you gonna do something with that pole between your legs?" Her words ended on a grunt as Kellen shifted and pushed up into her.

"Fuck, so tight," Kellen groaned.

Laikyn braced her hands on the cool tile, enjoying the feel of having Kellen finally filling her. Goddess, the male had tortured her with his hands. She moaned as he pulled out, swearing she could feel every vein and bump on his dick.

"I'm going to make you beg before I let you come." He powered into her from behind.

She had no doubt whatsoever he would and could do it, too. The question was who would come first?

She squeezed her inner muscles around him, making him groan. "Such a bad little wolf," he growled.

Unable to say anything else as he quickly powered into her with more force, hard and fast, slow, and easy, alternating his strokes, never letting her get used to what he was going to do. But each time was more delicious than the last. She kept her hands on the wall, taking everything he gave her, loving him. Giving him control of her body was like free falling, a chance at freedom that she didn't know she needed until that moment.

His hands tweaked her nipples, then his right hand slid down her stomach, between her thighs. His fingers smoothed over her mound, making her buck, and then gripped her clit between two firm digits, toying with her. "Oh, yes, harder."

It was such sweet torment it was hard to hold herself up on her hands, dropping to her elbows, the tile was cool on her forehead as she rested against it.

"You better brace yourself," Kellen whispered. His fingers circled her clit again and again, pinching and toying with it. Just when she was on the verge of coming, he'd stop, to her utter dismay.

She tried to ride his cock, rocking back against him, squeezing his dick each time he pushed back inside her. Kellen twisted her nipple, hard, doing the same with her clit. "You think to control our fucking?"

Her wolf snarled until he bit down on his mark, their connection getting stronger with each moment that passed. He pulled her back flush to his chest, his cock pistoning in and out of her with his arm around her shoulders, anchoring her to him, the other he worked her clit.

"Kellen, please," she begged, biting his arm to keep from screaming.

"Yes. That's exactly what I wanted to hear," he growled.

White hot pleasure washed over her under his touch. "Can I come now?"

His fingers stilled on her clit. "Yes, Mon Chaton. I want to feel you. Come all you want."

She lost herself to the pleasure Kellen gave her.

Kellen roared behind her. The animalistic sound spurred her on. His cock swelling inside her was followed by his come jetting. A spasm shook her with each release of his come he spent deep within her, and then he bit down on the meaty part of her shoulder where he'd placed his mark, making her come again.

Too hoarse to shout, she whispered his name. Her forehead now resting on the back of her hands, her throat dry and raw from her screams of ecstasy.

"Damn, baby." Kellen licked her. His rough voice making her shiver.

Laughing, she turned to look, meeting his blue eyes. "The water is cold."

He pulled out, sighing deeply. "Gonna need to buy a bigger water heater."

She felt warm and happy in his arms, but then he moved, and the cold water hit her. "Can't you make it warm, now?"

Dark brows winged up. "I'm not a magician, baby."

They quickly washed up before hurrying out of the icy shower, dressing in record time.

"You want to wait in here while I take care of club business, or come with me," Kellen asked pulling his boots back on while he sat in the large leather recliner.

Laikyn looked around the office her mate considered his domain. "I'll wait in here. I'm sort of tired."

Kellen got to his feet as he drew her close, making her sigh deeply. Her heart clenched, and she realized she was finally where she should be. With her mate. Tears stung her eyes.

"What's wrong?" Kellen lifted her chin.

"Nothing. I'm happy." She blinked away the moisture from her eyes.

"Me too, baby. Why don't you take a nap? I'll make sure nobody fucks with you or comes in here except for me." He brushed a gentle kiss over her lips.

She grinned. "You wore me out."

"Hello, my recently doing the deed wolfies. Am I interrupting a moment? I hate when I interrupt moments," Jennaveve muttered. "I almost interrupted a moment earlier, but I backed away real quiet like, and from the looks of it, neither of you noticed, so I'd say I succeeded. Anyhoo, I really must be going, and wanted to say bye. It's rude not to say goodbye, you know." She glared at Laikyn and then Kellen.

Laikyn bit her lip to keep from laughing. "Um, you're leaving?"

"Bye," Kellen said.

Laikyn smacked Kellen's bicep. "Do you need a ride or us to call someone?"

"Rude boy. You need to learn some manners. Don't you know you should treat your elders with more respect?" Jennaveve stood straighter, her petite frame vibrating with power.

"My apologies. How can I be of assistance?"

Jennaveve clapped. "Can I drive your vehicle?"

"No," Kellen barked.

"Tone, rude one. You asked what you could do, and I ask for a tiny little thing. Goddess, you'd think I asked for your first born or something." She tossed her hands in the air. "Which, by the way, will be just like his father." She winked at Laikyn.

It was instinct that had Laikyn pressing her hand to her stomach and then searching inside herself. She didn't feel any different.

"Not yet, Laikyn dear. It's too soon. Now, about me driving your big car." Turquoise eyes stared straight at Kellen.

Kellen looked like he was ready to bust a blood vessel. "My XV is not a car, or a toy. Do you need a lift back to Mystic?"

She blinked, a cute pout on her full lips. Laikyn would have sworn the female was crazy. Hell, she may be, but she'd shown them a lot while they'd allowed her entry into their minds. Now, she was sure she would be more prepared when and if they were attacked again.

"You wolves are so easy to mess with. Especially you alphas and your toys." The Fey laughed. "Now, you need to keep your head straight. I was truly able to slip right in unnoticed and got quite an eyeful of the two of you in the shower. I mean, eye bleach is on the shopping list now, thank you very much. It's a blessing you were not hitting the, *you know what hole.* I'm not sure my poor ole heart could have handled that."

"Can I eat her now," Kellen begged Laikyn.

Laikyn knew her face had to be as red as a hot tamale candy, but she had to keep her mate from following through on his threat. "Jennaveve, you really shouldn't spy on people. It's rude."

"See, so easy to mess with you," Jennaveve tsked. "Once I realized what you were about, I left as quickly as I came," she snorted.

Laikyn held her hand up. "Don't say it or I will bite you."

Jennaveve frowned, but mirth lit her eyes. "You have a link to me, now. If you have need, all you gotta do is reach out, and I'll be here in a blink."

Kellen opened his mouth, but before a word came out, the little Fey was gone. "That is freaky as shit."

She had to agree. "Go on, finish your tasks. I'll be fine."

"Who's the boss here?" Kellen crowded into her space.

Placing her hands on his chest, Laikyn stared up at him. His muscles flexed under her fingers. He truly was too damn sexy for words. With his dark hair and blue eyes, lips that were full and oh so kissable she couldn't help but lean forward and kiss him. When he took the kiss over, she wanted to remove their clothes and forget all about club and pack business. "You are."

He nodded and rested his palms on her hips. "I'll hurry. Get some rest while you can. I have plans for the next few hours." Lowering his head, he kissed her hungrily.

Jennaveve shook her head as she watched the Iron Wolves from her treehouse. "Silly men."

"How was your trip, Jenna?" Talia asked.

Looking at the Fey who'd been rescued from her abusive shifter husband, Jenna decided to not tell her where she'd been. The younger female had a lot of healing left to do. Her daughter would help in that regard, but Jenna's job was to also oversee her charges. Some would say she took her job too seriously, but she was bored. At her age she needed a little excitement, and the call from the wolves was just what she'd needed. At her age, she took what pleasure she could.

"Earth to Jennaveve."

Fingers snapping in front of her irritated the ever-loving crap out of her. "Talia, do you want to keep those fingers?"

Seeing fear wash over her new friend, made Jenna instantly regret her words. "You know I'd never hurt you. I didn't mean I'd physically take your fingers away." She hurried to explain.

"Of course, you didn't" Talia's words didn't match her actions.

With a sigh, Jenna grabbed onto one of the weaker Fey's hands, showing her the truth of her words. At the same time, she poured healing strength into Talia, something she hadn't done often because the stubborn female wouldn't open up. Now, her mind, body, and soul welcomed Jenna and her healing powers. Like a sponge she sucked in the goodness she offered.

Weak, Jenna fell backward.

"What have you done?" Talia cried.

Shaking her head, Jenna struggled to her feet. "I just need a bit to recoup. Be a dear and fetch me some coffee."

Her mouth was drier than the Sahara Desert. She couldn't tell Talia that she'd taken too much, not when the young female before her hadn't realized what she was doing. Poor thing had been through so much.

She made it into her sanctuary, or her bedroom, the soothing gold and red tones immediately calmed her racing heart. The large sleigh bed with the mound of pillows beckoned her. With a thought, her clothes were gone, replaced with a long T-shirt. Her long hair hung loose, but she was too tired to worry about braiding it. By the time Talia returned with the requested coffee, Jenna had climbed up the two steps to her huge bed and was snuggled under the covers.

"Thank you, dear." Her voice sounded older to her own ears.

"Why did you do that?" Talia held the steaming mug of fresh brewed java out for Jenna.

The sweet scent of vanilla hit her nose. "Give me a drink, child." Jenna had never called another Fey that word. It tended to make them feel like they were children. To her they were. She was one of the first of their kind. One of the originals. And she was so damn tired. She took a long drink of the heavenly brew, finishing it in two long pulls.

"Sleep, Jennaveve. I'll be here when you wake."

Jenna rolled onto her side, intending to tell her to go, but darkness swept over her. She felt him searching, an oily substance with no heart, and no redeeming quality. He wanted more. Always more than what he had. Jenna sent a flash of bright white light into the blackness, a love so pure he had no choice but to recoil. Satisfied she'd be safe and so would her charges for the time being, she let herself take a calming breath. The Iron Wolves would need a Fey or two on their side, like the Mystic Wolves. She only needed to figure out how to break it to one of her charges, or two and send them on their way. Not that they couldn't come back to the Fey land anytime to recharge. Sighing, she rolled onto her stomach, and finally, once she realized she had several solutions, she slept. Kellen Styles was such fun to mess with. She'd have to make sure she accompanied the Fey she sent.

Chapter Thirteen

Laikyn jerked awake. She had a sinking sensation something wasn't right and wished Kellen hadn't made his office noise proof. Blinking sleep from her eyes, she sat the recliner back up. She'd thought of lying on one of the sofas but chose Kellen's chair. With his scent permeating the large leather piece, her wolf had whined as she'd walked past it. If she was totally honest, the female wanted to roll around in his scent as well.

Now, she wished the male was here so she could be reassured the sinking feeling was nothing but a left-over dread from before. The light from the bathroom lit up only part of the space, but her shifter sight allowed her to see clearly. Her enhanced hearing didn't pick up anything other than her own heartbeat. "Calm down," she muttered to herself.

Getting to her feet, Laikyn tried to take a step, but the floor, which was made of concrete, became a muddy mess. The feeling of sinking several inches made her yell out, and she tried to launch herself back into the chair, only to find herself surrounded by woods and trees. Panic threatened to choke her. Through their mate link she shouted for Kellen but came up against a wall.

She looked around her surroundings, wondering where she was. The tall trees looked like the ones near her home, but the thick mud didn't make sense since they hadn't had any hard rain in a long while. Even when they did, she couldn't remember a time when it was ever like a mud pit. Then she remembered what the Cordells had said and tried to picture herself back inside the club.

An unholy laugh had her spinning in a circle. Darkness still surrounded her, but at least she was no longer stuck.

"Ah, you think to get away again, little girl?" A voice with a thick accent came from all around her.

Laikyn's wolf wanted to come out and run, but in her shifted form she wasn't as logical. She used the logic that Jenna had shown them and tapped into the power the Fey had shown was inside all shifters. She'd been a quick study her entire life and hoped this time would be no different. Closing her eyes, she pictured herself in a room surrounded by friends, and Kellen. The Iron Wolves club expressly. Laikyn did everything she was told to do. When she heard the cackling voice, she almost gave up and started running, but kept pouring all her resolve in the image, until finally she felt the wind blowing past her face. Pain seared her arm, but she kept the image firmly in her mind, even when she saw blood red eyes, and the face of the devil staring back at her.

"You can't escape me. I'm too powerful," he roared.

Again, she kept her focus, and then in a blink she found herself in the middle of the dance floor of the Iron Wolves, blood dripping down her arm.

"Laikyn, what the fuck is going on?"

"Kellen," her voice breaking. All her strength gave out on that one word, and then her world began to spin.

"It's alright. I've got you." Kellen's scent and arms enclosed her in their familiar warmth. "Where did you come from?"

She tried to think past the pain in her arm, but the burning sensation became worse than anything she'd ever experienced. "My arm... hurts."

Her mate looked at the bleeding mess. "Who did this?" He brought his nose close to the oozing wound. A deep growl rumbled from his chest. "I will kill the bastard."

"Please, take me to the clinic and I'll show you how to help me." She couldn't raise her hand even as she tried to caress his cheek.

"Call the Fey back," Kellen ordered.

In his usual commanding way, the big bad alpha wasn't stopping to realize he could reach out with his mind. Laikyn wished she had the strength to try herself, but the amount of energy she'd spent getting away from the vampire was more than she had ever used. "Call Damien and Lucas. Tell them he's here. Please," she begged.

"Xan, call the asshats. Their numbers," Kellen stopped speaking.

Laikyn couldn't see Xan, but through her and Kellen's link felt the other male reaching out to Kellen. Again, she wished her body wasn't so weak. Never in her entire life had she been so drained.

"Why is this cut draining me so?" She blinked up at Kellen.

They reached the small area set up for injured members. "I'd say it's due to you moving from one place to another like you did, the way Jennaveve does. We are shifters with a touch of Fey, so it's more taxing on us than them. Now, let me look at your wound, and order me around, Mon Chaton. This will be what we call your free pass." She saw the strain around his eyes and wanted to ease it.

"I'm going to be fine. Truly." After pointing out the different things he needed to clean her wound, Kellen and Laikyn sat on the large bed while they waited for Xan to arrive. She explained how she'd fallen asleep in his office, only to wake in the forest.

He cleansed the wound, flinching each time she did, making her aware how much it pained him to see her hurt.

"Close your eyes, baby. Nobody will take you away on my watch."

Laikyn's body wouldn't allow her to, even with Kellen's large body next to hers. The grating voice and red eyes looming out at her kept her body tense and awake. "I can't." She squeezed his hand.

Kellen lay down, pulling her onto his chest. "Open your mind to me. I promise, ain't nobody or anything gonna mind fuck you again."

The soothing growl, and yes, she thought all his tones were wonderful. "I love you." Laikyn yawned. With her mate firmly in her head, his presence soothing the wounds of her mind, she found it easy to let go.

He kept his anger hidden behind a wall of steel, being sure only love poured forth, shielding Laikyn in comfort.

Xan's light steps, along with his mate's came to him long before they entered. "*Laikyn is sleeping. Did you get ahold of the Cordell brothers?*"

"*They will be here shortly. They have a private jet.*" Xan's grunt of disapproval through their link made Kellen smile.

"*They're old as fuck, of course they have a jet.*" He had no hard feelings toward the twins. Well, not much since his mate didn't want either man.

"You two can quit talking with your inside voices. I'm awake and feel much better." Laikyn looked up at Kellen.

He kept her from sliding off him with a firm hand on her rounded ass, much to her dismay. "Stay," he murmured.

"Kellen, you have things to do and so do I. We can't just lay around. Besides, I need to pee."

Xan laughed. "I don't think you can do that for her, big guy."

"I'll carry you." Kellen sat up with Laikyn in his arms.

She growled. "You will do no such thing." Pointing to the door not five feet from them. "I'll be right through there. What do you think could happen? Besides, I'm awake, and prepared. I know what happened now. I realize why he was able to get to me. It won't happen again."

"Breezy, go with her. And no arguments. I know you women always go to the bathroom together, so it's no hardship." Kellen let Laikyn slide down his body, ignoring his hard-on. The damn thing was in a constant state of arousal around his female.

Xan shrugged. "It's true. We've studied the phenomena of you females, and still don't understand why you go in groups to the lady's room. Now, go on and make it quick. My wolf doesn't like you out of its sight right now."

"Aw, you are such a sweet talker. Tell your wolf my wolf says she loves him, too." Breezy kissed Xan before grabbing Laikyn's hand.

Kellen shook his head. "Who is the boss of that relationship?"

Looking at the two women's retreating backs, Xan adjusted his own erection. "Need I say more?"

"Fucking pussy whipped." Kellen ran his hand over his jaw, feeling the scrape of his beard. "That was some freaky-ass-shit out there earlier. How the hell do we combat what we can't see?"

The worry and fear he'd kept hidden from Laikyn poured out of his mouth.

Xan stared at Kellen, then moved closer. "We do what we've always done. We protect the weaker ones, then we hunt the motherfucker down, and kill him. Not necessarily in that order. Your mate showed great strength, and knowledge that we all need by moving through whatever way the Fey do. We need to tap into that if we are going to defeat him."

"It drained her to the point of collapse. The members of our pack who aren't as strong could die if they used such power. I won't lose anyone, no matter what their rank is until we know more about this new skill set. Hell, I don't even know if it's ours to use. Laikyn is... special. She's one of the smartest of our kind." He stopped at the chuckle coming from his best friend.

"You are so pussy whipped." Xan jumped back as Kellen swiped his fist toward him.

Shaking his head, Kellen began to pace. "You tell anybody, and I'll beat your ass. But you know what I mean. She's always learned things faster than others. What's that memory called?" He turned back to face his second, seeing Breezy and Laikyn standing in the doorway.

"Eidetic memory," Breezy answered.

Laikyn gasped. "How the heck do you know that?"

"Everyone knows. Do you know it's very rare? I wasn't sure exactly what that meant until watching The Big Bang Theory. One of the main characters has the same thing, only you are nothing like him."

"I love that show. Sheldon is hilarious, but I agree with you. I am nothing like him. Or at least I hope I'm not." She walked up to Kellen.

He looked down at her, wondering who the women were talking about.

"You clearly don't watch much television, do you?" Laikyn snuggled into his arms, making him forget all about television.

"Not really, no. I'll watch movies, but don't have time for watching things on TV at home unless it's a movie without commercials. When I'm home, I'd rather do something constructive. Now that I have a mate, I think there's lots of things I'd rather do with my spare time." He gripped her ass, letting her feel exactly what he meant.

Breezy coughed. "No PDA. There are people in the room."

"You and Xan don't count. Besides, I am only hugging my mate."

"No, your dick is saying hello. Put that thing away. We have company." Xan tilted his head toward the door.

Kellen sensed their presence long before Xan had mentioned it but didn't want Laikyn to freeze up on him. Besides, he liked having her in his arms, smelling like him, and aroused.

"I'm aware," he answered without letting Laikyn go.

A hard knock on the door leading from the outside broke through the silence.

"Come in, Coti." The big Hawaiian led Damien and Lucas in. Both men looked at Laikyn, their eyes took in her injury, then stared at Kellen.

"What happened," Damien waved toward Laikyn.

Grinding his teeth, Kellen looked at Laikyn. "Do you want to tell them or me?"

"I will. Although, it might be easier if I showed them." She glanced over her shoulder, asking him for permission.

Goddess, he was a lucky bastard. With a nod, he entered her mind. *I will do this with you so there is no fucked up shit going on. If you feel threatened, you back out and I'll kill them both.*

"Okay." And just like that his mate soothed him.

"We will allow that and understand if you will be piggybacking in with her, Mr. Styles." Damien gave a regal nod.

"I'll be with her every step of the way. You understand I will gut you both if you try anything stupid, right?"

"Pup, if we were going to try anything stupid, do you think we'd be standing in this... place, offering assistance?" Lucas spoke for the first time.

They weren't identical twins but close enough it was hard for most to tell, who was who. However, Kellen could tell the difference in them by their scents. He focused on Damien, realizing he was the leader.

Power flowed from Lucas. "We are equal, pup. Never forget it."

Kellen allowed his own energy to flow, forcing the other male to stagger back. He placed Laikyn behind him. "Don't come at me with your shit, boy. You and your brother may know more about this thing we are facing, but I can and will wipe the floor with you."

Lyric pushed her way into the room. "Alright guys. Put your dicks away. No need to piss all over the place."

"For the love of all, woman," Rowan roared. "Will you stop running into rooms full of testosterone."

Like a bubble that had a pin pushed into it, the air thinned out of the room.

"Your mate is correct. Laikyn. Please show us what happened so we may be of assistance." Damien placed his hand on Lucas's shoulder.

They may be fraternal twins who were more the same than not, and had equal strengths, but their temperaments were very different. One light and one dark. Kellen made note of his observations, bringing Laikyn to stand in front of him. With his arms banding about her waist, he brought his lips close to her ear. "Let's do this and get it over with."

"I didn't see his face, and his voice may not be real." She tried to reassure them, making Kellen want to kill the bastard even more for what he'd tried to do.

"We understand, and believe us, we will know who and what we are facing through your memories. Trust us." Lucas's eyes focused on Kellen. The other man's pupil expanded, swallowing up his entire eye.

Linking with Laikyn, they opened up and instead of letting the Cordells into her memories, they flowed into a space in between. Kellen stared around the void, wondering where they hell they were, until Damien's form appeared. *"This is an in-between where we are all safe from each other's invasion of privacy."*

"Meaning you don't have a direct line to our minds?" Kellen wanted to be clear.

Lucas rolled his eyes. *"We will now as do you, have a link to each of us. However, you can sever it the same as us. Now, let's get on with the showing and less talking. Your voice is getting on my last damn nerve."*

"How have you not killed him before now," Kellen asked Damien.

The other male shrugged his shoulders. In the space they'd come, Kellen looked at each man, seeing they'd chosen different clothing than they'd had on in the real world.

"This is what we are most comfortable in." Damien indicated the loose-fitting shirt and pants that could have come from any era.

Kellen glanced at his own jeans and T, then shrugged. "Show them, Mon Chaton."

Laikyn let her breath out, then allowed her mind to open, the images along with her fear flowed into all three of them. Kellen kept his beast at bay, barely. Damien and Lucas stood straight, their eyes doing that freaky thing with their pupils, their chests expanded once, twice, then he didn't think either male breathed for a full two minutes. When Laikyn finished showing them, minutes had passed. Neither Cordell made a move. Not a muscle or twitch of movement came from either of them. Almost as if they were no longer in their own bodies. Kellen held Laikyn closer. Neither of them making a sound in case it would break into whatever trance-like state they were in.

Lucas was the first to take a deep breath, followed by Damien. His eyes speared straight into Kellen's. "This was the work of a vampire, but not one as old as we'd first thought."

"He's the one from Kansas City. I'm afraid to say he's much more dangerous than just an old one, Lake. For our entire lives, we've heard of those who... take what they shouldn't, in order to gain more power. Lucas and I are old and have the blood of our ancestors flowing through our veins. That makes us very powerful. If someone was lucky enough to kill us, they'd be able to siphon off some of our strengths. Of course, there are other beings we could take from and gather power from, but it has been outlawed for centuries. Which is why we were hesitant to approach Laikyn, even though we thought she was our... anyway, that is in the past. Vampires have one shot at finding our Hearts Love. Many settle for something close, but with us, it is *one female for us both. We know now that there is only one who will complete us." He turned sad eyes away from Kellen, but he'd seen the longing.*

Pity, for the brothers had Kellen understanding their plight. "What did you find out, other than he was the same being? Can you track him before he attacks again?"

Damien flicked an imaginary piece of lint from his white shirt. "Leave him to us. We will handle the problem."

Kellen growled. "Listen, while I appreciate you and your brother rushing here and your offer of assistance, the fact remains, this is now pack business. We need to know how to fight this new threat."

Lucas's eyes turned an eerie red, similar to what Laikyn had showed them in her mind. "You are like him," she whispered, hand flying to her mouth.

"We are nothing like him, yet we are similar, which is why you must leave him to us. You want to help, then stay out of our way. This is council

business. We've already reported what you showed us to our father, who is the Vampire King."

"Well, fuck me runnin," Kellen swore.

"What? Now that you know you're dealing with royalty, are you going to treat us with respect?" Laughter lit the man's eyes. If they'd met at a different time, under different circumstances, Kellen may have liked the man.

"I don't think we'd have hung out in the same circles, but I would have hired you to pimp my ride or something," Damien said.

Kellen moved Laikyn beside him, freeing up his right hand. "Sit and spin boys. We done here?" He raised his middle finger.

Lucas shook his head. "See, I told you I liked him."

"That's because he's more like you." Damien pushed at Lucas's shoulder.

"What's that supposed to mean?" Lucas asked.

While the two brothers went about a shoving match, Kellen stared at his mate. "Let's leave the *two dickheads to fight it out. I need to be balls deep inside you."*

Two masculine groans met his words. "Inside voice." Followed by, "TMI," was shouted out by Damien and Lucas in unison. Kellen wasn't sure who said what.

"Damn, I was just getting ready to shake the shit out of you," Xan said, standing next to the large bed, a worried frown on his face.

Kellen stared at Laikyn lying next to him. "How the hell did we end up here?" The two vampires sat in chairs across the room.

Xan shrugged his massive shoulders. "After about fifteen minutes of y'all standing around looking like you were in the zone, I got a little freaked, and lifted you up first, put you here, then placed Laikyn next to you. I felt a little bad for the Cordells, so I sat them down. Breezy promised me she'd give me a treat later, so all's good. No need to thank me."

Laikyn sat up, rubbing her eyes. "Do I want to know?"

He explained to her how they'd ended up in bed, leaving out the thank you Xan was expecting from his mate.

Damien and Lucas both popped out of the chairs in fighting stances. Damien spoke first. "What the hell? How long were we gone?"

"About thirty minutes." Breezy looked at the clock on the wall, then nodded.

"Times a wasting. He's probably already out hunting. I'd say what he did depleted his reserves. It takes great strength to move a person without their help or consent. Which means there is going to be a body count. We can track him by those, or we can go hunting. I vote for hunting," Lucas said.

"The vision you showed us, that was your home, or at least the woods near your family home?" Damien asked Laikyn.

Laikyn bit her lip, nodding. "I haven't lived there in a couple years, but yeah. My parents have a home in Florida, but still own the property and the house here and come back often. They always hoped I'd move back here."

Kellen kept his anger at the thought of her living out there all alone to himself.

"We will go there now and see if he's there or been there." Lucas held his hand up. "If you go with us, he will feel your presence and run. Us, he will think we are checking up on him, and think to one up us. Believe me, we've faced vampires like him."

Kellen understood what they were saying, but having others out protecting his pack, defending his mate grated. He wanted to be the one to rip this vampire's throat out with his teeth.

"The Council will want him to face them. I can't allow you to kill him outright unless he actually harms you or your mate. I know he did do that." He pointed at the healed wound. "But he could have killed her. Instead, he was trying to capture her. Believe me when I say this being is not one to play with. Allow us to handle him, and when the time comes to see his death, I will petition you to be there."

"If he threatens my mate, or any of my pack, I will kill him. Your Council be damned." Kellen stood from the bed.

Damien inclined his head. In a blink, he and Lucas were gone.

"Well, that is some freaky ass shit," Lyric gasped.

"You can say that again," Rowan agreed.

Chapter Fourteen

Damien and Lucas landed in the yard of Laikyn's family home. Her scent still loomed around them, but the vampire they were hunting overlaid everything.

"He's been here and gone. We can trace him, but I think we'll be chasing shadows. He's got to have some donors around that he's left alive. Let's find them, and then we'll find him." Lucas bent and picked up a piece of dirt, signs of several footprints were present.

"We should split up. I'll follow his trail, while you see if you can't get a lock on one of the humans that he has working for him," Damien murmured, staring at the home.

Lucas looked at the sky, the sun rising would work in their favor. One thing they'd learned in all their very long years, was not to underestimate an enemy. "Maybe we should stick together until the sun is at its highest. Who knows what kind of nasty surprises this being has in store for us." He tilted his head toward the home. A feeling of being watched even though they couldn't sense a presence was strong.

"Don't you feel that?" Lucas asked through *their twin bond.*

Damien turned his back, pretending to study the gravel drive, Lucas was sure. *"There is something, but I thought it was my overactive imagination."*

"Let us take to the sky as air, and circle back. See if whatever it is shows its hand." Lucas followed Damien, becoming molecules.

A crack split the ground they'd been standing on moments later. Both brothers floated higher, waiting to see what happened next as a male came out the door, followed by another. Lucas didn't recognize either one, but the fact they were newly made vampires, or younger than a century, had him amazed they were able to control their powers. Not to mention they were working together. Damn, they needed to inform the Council of Vampires.

313

"We need to talk to mom and dad." Damien's words echoed his thoughts.

Before Lucas could agree, wind whipped past them. He and his brother knew it was the beings below searching for a sign. They kept their cool, neither of them young and inexperienced fighters, although their instincts demanded they return to the ground and kill the puppets.

"They will lead us to him." Lucas floated next to Damien.

His brother's dry chuckle entered his head. *"What's that saying? Like shooting fish in a barrel?"*

"Yeah, well right now we're like sitting ducks." Lucas grit his teeth as the two shits below used what powers they had, aiming cracks of lightning at them. The slight stings felt like the pinching he'd endured as a child from the little females who he and Damien could give two shits about.

"In another five minutes they'll have to give up and head toward their master," Damien grunted.

What felt like more than an hour later, the men below stopped attacking the skies in the hopes of ferreting out Damien and Lucas. Their voices carrying in the wind.

"Do you think the boss man was wrong, and we were just tossing our power around for nothing?" One of the men said, sounding winded.

The younger of the two shrugged massive shoulders. "Who knows, and who cares. We had a job to do, and we did it. You saw those men just as I did. Now, we can tell Mr. Watson we scared the baddies off, and maybe be rewarded."

Unholy glee entered both men's eyes that even the distance couldn't diminish. Lucas focused on the one who'd spoken last and eased into his mind. The things both were guilty of since their turning gave them a death sentence. They wouldn't need approval of the Council for taking the bastards lives. He forwarded the images to his father, knowing Damien was seeing it as well. The sight of Nigel Watson performing blood rituals gave him pause, which tipped the vampire off that something wasn't right, and had him spinning in a circle.

"What the hell is wrong with you, Ron?" The older vampire questioned.

Ron rubbed his temple. "I think I expended too much. Let's go before the sun rises."

Having formed a link with the soon to be dusted man, Lucas allowed them to leave.

"Did you go into the other's mind?" Lucas asked.

"Yeah, it's not pretty. He's been tried and found guilty as well."

After the sun was up for a good fifteen minutes, they floated down to the ground. Laikyn's home had been used by the men, but they were hoping it wasn't trashed. If it had been, they'd be sure and return it to an even better condition. No way would they allow those abominations to sour the shifters minds to their kind.

"You do know she's not ours, right?" Damien smirked over his shoulder.

With a glare, Lucas opened his senses to make sure there weren't any more surprises waiting inside the home. His brother's comment didn't sting the way he'd thought it would, meaning neither of them were nearly as invested in the she-wolf.

"We need to get out more, brother." Lucas walked up behind Damien once they were sure the home was secure.

Inside was only slightly messed up. Had they been human, the fact someone had been there would have gone completely unnoticed. Shifters would have smelled the funk long before even Damien and Lucas being half-breeds.

"Really? Funk?" Damien raised his eyebrow.

"They smell like rotting cabbage. Who the hell likes that stuff?" Lucas walked to the fireplace, staring at the pictures lining the mantel.

"Don't touch anything," his brother's growl came before he could touch the family portrait. "Let's just see if there are any clues of the vamps, and then get out of here."

The need to eliminate the threat and then leave, rode them both hard.

Taking to the skies again, they had a direction, and a better idea of where to look. With the vampires traveling in packs, Lucas and Damien stayed close together even in the daylight. "Did you pass the information we learned to the alpha?"

Damien's eyes cut to him as he mentioned the other man. "I thought you did?"

Opening the link to Kellen, he waited politely, a term many didn't equate with Damien and him, and then gave him the latest news.

"They were in my mate's family home?" Kellen's tone became what Lucas called deadly.

"There were only two there when we arrived, but we smelled the master and several others. Her home wasn't destroyed, yet the stink was offensive to our nose. You full bloods would have been able to smell them long before us, and vice versa. We left things as they were since they hadn't destroyed it, and in case they returned we didn't want them to

know we were on to them. However, if they do damage anything we will replace and or repair."

"Did you kill them?" Laikyn's sweet voice interrupted his reassurance.

Shaking his head, he pinched the bridge of his nose. "Again, we couldn't, or we would have tipped our hand. They are our lead to the master."

"When you find him, I want to be the one to end him, Cordell." Kellen didn't ask.

Damien looked at Lucas but let him take the lead. "Mr. Styles, I'm afraid, until he does damage to you or yours, he is ours to take care of. He's broken the laws of our kind."

"What the ever-loving fuck does that mean?"

He could imagine the alpha was ready to rip his throat out. Lucas stared at Damien, then shrugged. "Meaning, until the time comes where the crimes against one of your pack is more heinous than that of ours, my brother and I will be taking Nigel Watson before our King. There I can promise you he will see his end, along with those who are following him."

The growl that came through would have had lesser men pissing in their pants. Damien and Lucas had faced bigger beasts and lived to tell the tale. "We understand you're upset, but these are our laws."

"Screw your laws. If that fucker shows his fangs near me or mine, I don't give no fucks about you and your king. I will kill him and all who stand in my way," Kellen said.

Lucas nodded even though Kellen wouldn't be able to see. "I would be disappointed if you didn't. Rest assured we hunt him while he sleeps, so the chance of him coming at you again is slim."

A grunt was his answer before the connection was cut.

"Well, that was fun." Lucas glared at his brother who was chuckling.

"Hey, I would have been the one to reach out, but he seemed to like you better."

Kellen didn't like anyone other than his people, and now Damien and Lucas were so far off his like list, Lucas and his brother would need to go in with full armor. Again, it wouldn't be the first time they had to do so.

His brother's chuckle had him bumping him in the air. They began their descent to the ground, coming in slowly to the rock cave where the two vampires they'd tracked had disappeared into. Opening his senses, he found several other beings inside the cavern, along with the being they came for.

Hitting the ground, he and Damien shifted to their wolven form when a large net fell out of the tree, trapping them both. Lucas tried to shift back to molecules, quickly realizing the netting was made of silver. His wolf whined as the harsh metal bit into his fur.

Damien rolled out from under the enclosure, only part of his body having been trapped beneath. He lay panting from pain, his dark eyes stared at Lucas. "*I will get help.*"

Lucas tried to get up onto all fours, but the weight of the net, combined with the silver, made it impossible. "*Call out to Kellen.*"

His last sight was of Damien shifting to his human form, and then darkness took him.

Kellen felt the mental knocking again from the Cordell twins. His first thought was to ignore the men. Anger at the bullshit they had given him about their rules of taking the man, who had tried to take his mate before their Council, ate at him. A vision of an injured wolf trapped beneath a silver netting had him bolting upright.

"The vampire has set a trap. Lucas is injured and if I don't get him free, he will die."

He couldn't ignore the plea from Damien any more than he could from one of his own. *"Where are you?"*

As Damien showed Kellen where they'd flown, his body froze. They were closer to Rowan's home. Through the pack link, he sent the info to Rowan and Xan, unsure where the men were. He'd been sure all the pack were staying within the compound, but he'd taken his mate to his home. Now, he wanted to kick himself.

"We are at the club, along with Xan and Breezy. I just checked my security footage, and nothing is showing up, not even a tree has been trampled." Rowan assured him.

Kellen shook his head, wondering why the male thought trees would be torn down, but didn't ask. *"I want everyone to stay at the club, and don't let any strangers in. Period. I'm bringing Laikyn back, and then I'm taking Coti and Wyck with me. The Cordells are in trouble."*

"I'll go with you," Rowan said.

"No, I need you and Xan to protect our mates." Kellen held Laikyn closer.

"You're the alpha, aren't you more important than me?"

His mate whimpered.

"I'm the alpha, and I make the rules. Protect my mate like you would yours." Kellen cut the connection with Xan and Rowan.

"I'm going to need you to be the mate to the alpha and show everyone you're strong. You need to lead the women, like I lead the men. Can you do that for me, Mon Chaton?"

"It's not fair. We just got together. What if—" she stopped on a cry.

"Have you so little faith in me?" He lifted her into his arms, striding out to the garage and his XV, wishing he had time to reassure her.

Laikyn wrapped her arms around his shoulders. "No, I just hate that I brought this here. It's my fault."

Kellen placed his mate in the passenger seat, gripping her chin in his fingers. "When I get you back home, I'm going to have to teach you a lesson on placing blame where it belongs." He bent and took her mouth in a hard kiss. Her flavor exploded in his mouth, making his wolf demand more.

"Promises promises," Laikyn whispered when he let her up for air.

"Buckle up, baby." Kellen shut the door, then hurried around to the driver's side. He could have shifted and reached the vampires quicker, but he wasn't leaving his mate unprotected.

The drive to the club was made in silence, his hand holding Laikyn's. Wyck and Coti stood outside, their bodies tense. He pulled close to the door and was pleased when his mate waited for him to come around to her side. "I love you. When I close my eyes, it's you I see. You're in my soul. Without you, I'd wither up and die. Stay safe for me, Laikyn."

Tears welled in her eyes. "You are a romantic at heart, Kellen Styles."

"Only for you. Now, if you don't get your fine ass in that building and stay safe, I will turn you over my knee, and you won't be able to sit for days without thinking of me." He opened the door.

"Great, now everyone is gonna smell my arousal." She laughed, wiping a stray tear.

"Go on. I'd rather them smell that than your sadness." Kellen tapped her heart shaped ass.

She gave a little yelp, turning at the door to glare at Coti and Wyck. "Keep your alpha safe above all else."

The two large men nodded, then they all shifted seamlessly.

"I love you, Kellen."

He trotted over and butted her until she was inside with Rowan at the door making sure he shut and locked them inside. No words were needed.

Although in human form both Coti and Wyck were much bigger than him, in their shifted forms, Kellen actually was larger than all of them. He didn't question the semantics, assuming it was due to him being the alpha, but racing off with the two largest wolves of his pack, Kellen knew they were a force to be reckoned with.

Their paws ate up the ground, ears, and eyes open for anything out of the ordinary. Kellen knew the woods surrounding his land like the back of his hand. Nearing the spot Damien had shown them, they slowed a few miles out, smells filtering through their senses. His nose was the first to pick up on the rotting foliage, something that shouldn't be happening in such a lush environment. He indicated through their link to both men with him to slow and then stop, showing what he saw.

In their wolven form colors weren't as vivid, so Kellen shifted back to human while Coti and Wyck kept guard. He didn't have to walk far before finding what was causing the smell. Several bodies lay discarded, drained of blood.

"These look like fresh kills," Kellen said.

"Why do they smell like rotten eggs?" Wyck's tone was one of disgust.

Kellen had no answer and didn't want to stick around to find out. *"Don't disturb the bodies. Let's circle around them. The Cordells are about a half mile from here."*

He showed them the caves in their mind in case they had to split up. Kellen shifted back, leading the way around the dozen dead men who'd been the vampires' meal.

"I see the wolf in the net. Are you sure this isn't a trap for all of us?" Wyck never one to trust easily raised his head to the sky, inhaled deeply.

Kellen knew the other brother was near and waited patiently. Moments passed and then Damien solidified before him. Kellen shifted to human as well.

"Neat trick. Why didn't he do that?" Kellen nodded toward Lucas who lay panting, his eyes looking pained.

"We have the same reaction to silver as you. Why did you not bring anything to remove the net?" Damien looked around Kellen.

"Don't question me, boy. I have a plan, but I wasn't risking my people. Besides, do you see a vehicle trail around here?" He held his arms out to his sides and spun in a circle. "I'd say your friends had the one trap, and maybe more inside if you'd have made it further. Now, we can stand out here and have a pissing contest, or I can head to Rowan's and be back with what we need. His home is on the other side of these caves."

Damien hung his head. "I'm sorry."

"I bet that hurt," Kellen taunted, but didn't wait to hear anymore. He walked over to the downed wolf. "Hang in there, I'll be back and get you out of there."

A vision of the kid in the hospital flashed in his head. He wondered if they'd need to call Jennaveve to help this one, too. With a shrug, he shifted again, his body flowing into the big black beast without any of the repercussions the rest of the pack would suffer. It was good to be alpha. He sent up a silent prayer to their goddess for her gifts.

Wyck and Coti kept pace with him, their attentions alert to any more traps the vampires may have set for intruders. They reached Rowan's and just to fuck with his newest member, Kellen looked at Wyck and gave a nod.

With a growl, Wyck took off at a full out run and knocked over a good-sized tree, knowing Rowan would be getting alerts on his phone.

"Why the hell would y'all do that to my poor tree?"

"We need you to open your garage so I can borrow a couple four-wheelers." Kellen barely kept from laughing as Rowan cursed up a blue streak.

"Kellen, that was so mean. You know he has issues," Lyric said.

"Yeah, control issues. It's too easy to fuck with him. Tell him we are scratching at his door, and if he doesn't let us in, we are gonna knock the fucker in."

The sound of several deadbolts disengaging kept him from messing with the ex-Navy SEAL.

"Thank you, Lyric."

"Hey, I let you in," Rowan growled.

"Yeah, but we like Lyric better."

Kellen and the others hopped on the two all-terrain vehicles Rowan had in the garage and hurried back to where they'd left Damien. Rowan really did like his toys to have all kinds of bells and whistles. With the log chain and winch attached Kellen hoped they could get the net off without damaging the wolf anymore.

Coming over the rise of the hill, he was glad to see no surprises waited for them, but the wolf looked even worse than before they'd left.

"Damien, will he be able to shift once we get the net off of him?"

Even though the other male wasn't anywhere to be seen, Kellen recognized the signature of his scent was still strong. Meaning he was there.

"How did you know?" Damien materialized.

Kellen looked over his shoulder, seeing the hybrid. "I'm a fast learner. Now answer the question. We're losing daylight."

"Depends. If he can, it'll be to human, not air."

"Let's do this, boys. Lucas, this is gonna hurt, cause we gotta drag it off you. I didn't have time or resources to bring in a crane to pull it from the top."

The wolf raised his head as much as he could.

"Lucas is aware and wants it done." Damien said between his teeth.

Looking between the two brothers, Kellen wondered if they shared the pain, but shrugged it off.

He hooked the winch up to the net, the silver stinging his palms. Jumping back onto the four-wheeler, Kellen grit his teeth and began driving forward. The net came off easily as they hadn't anchored it down, knowing the silver alone would hold them in place. Once he had it completely off, Damien dropped to his knees next to his brother, sweat dripping off his forehead.

"Can you shift?" Damien asked.

A painful whimper came from Lucas.

"Load him onto the back of here. Wyck will drive the other one while Coti runs next to us. Are you okay to disappear and fly back or do you want to ride with Wyck?"

Kellen didn't think the male was going to answer, but then he stood. "I'll ride with Wyck. Thank you."

"Let's roll out boys. Coti, don't stray too far from us. Stay on the same trail we came in on." Coti nodded then became his wolf again.

Kellen ripped the silver off the wench, tossing it aside. He and Wyck looked at Lucas, then lifted him together, laying him on the back of Kellen's borrowed four-wheeler. The big animal didn't make a sound, which worried him.

Wyck climbed back on his, with Damien on the back. They made tracks back to the club, but his worry for the injured wolf had him sending a call out to Jennaveve.

"Jennaveve. I hate to bother you again, but I have an injured um, wolf that could use some attention. I don't think he's going to last much longer." He sent her the image of the silver net lying over the wolf.

"I will be there shortly. Give me a bit. I see you are on the move. Where shall I come?"

He wondered at the weak tone but brushed it off as a matter of distance. *"The club. Thank you, Jennaveve."*

"You are most welcome, Alpha."

He was never so happy as he was when the large gates at the back of the club came into view. He loved the stylized image of the four claws. The Parker brothers stood by the gates, waiting to open them. Their eyes widened at the sight of the two men on the back, but they nodded then shut the gates.

Damn! How the hell did they go from one battle to the next?

He drove to the clinic doors. His mate's scent hit him hard. She clearly knew he was coming and with an injured person. His beast rose up, wanting to dump the male off. Kellen pushed back, knowing Laikyn loved him and only him.

"Come on. Let's get him inside." Kellen helped lift Lucas while Damien struggled to stand. "Did the silver affect you as well?"

Damien shook his head. "I'll be fine. I need to feed as does Lucas. And before you protest, no, I'm not asking. We will be fine until we can get donors."

Kellen walked into the clinic, turning sideways to enter with the large wolf. "What the hell does that mean?"

"Being hybrids we don't need blood to survive. Unless we're injured. Lucas will need some because he's in bad shape. I took some of his pain or he would have died." Damien shrugged.

Laikyn gasped. "Oh, my gawd. Put him down here. Breezy, get me as much blood as we have."

"What the hell." Damien looked around the room.

"This is a clinic of sorts for our kind. I'm still going to be practicing at the hospital, but we have everything that I'd need in emergencies here."

He watched his mate hook the wolf up with an IV, bag blood flowing into the animal while she cleaned his surface wounds. Then she turned to the other hybrid, pointing to a chair. He smiled as she ordered Damien to sit and then proceeded to give him his own pint of blood.

"Now, how long does it normally take before he can shift?"

Color began returning to Damien. The wolf on the table hadn't moved since they'd brought him in. All his wounds had been cleaned, and Laikyn had given him more blood.

The smell of honey and mint proceeded Jennaveve. "Oh, my word. What happened?"

Kellen watched Damien sit up straight, his dark eyes turned red. The wolf on the bed stirred, his eyes suddenly opened.

Jennaveve patted his head. "Don't you worry big guy. Jennaveve will get you right as rain." She placed her hand on his body, a silver and gold glow encompassed her and the wolf, streaks of color shot out, knocking Kellen and the others on their asses, and bringing Damien to his feet.

Kellen growled, tried to shift, and reach Laikyn.

He saw her head shake, then begin to crawl to him on all fours.

"What the hell is going on?" He asked.

"I don't know. That is not what happened when she healed Jared," Laikyn whispered.

Kellen pulled Laikyn onto his lap, the light from the trio getting brighter, then like a bulb bursting, it was gone.

"Who are you?" Jennaveve said, then collapsed into Damien's arms.

A very human and naked Lucas lay on the table. "Ours," he said with wonder.

Getting to his feet, Kellen put Laikyn behind him. "What did you do to her?"

The tiny Fey was held close to his chest, Damien looked stunned. "We didn't do anything. She did it. I've never," he stopped and swallowed. "What is she?"

He walked over to Jennaveve, ignoring the growling pair. "She is Fey and part of my pack."

Chapter Fifteen

Laikyn knew she had to diffuse the situation and fast. Jennaveve was to the Cordells what she was to Kellen. Her stubborn mate had to see that.

"Listen, guys. I think you should let me check on her."

Damien held her closer. "We will see to her well-being."

A deep rumble shook the building. "They have come." Lucas said.

Fear hit her. Hard. "What can we do?"

Lucas closed his eyes. "My father is coming. Be prepared. He is kind of an arrogant—"

"I wouldn't finish that if I was you. Is this your mate?" The extremely tall man, sized Laikyn up and down with one glance.

Holy shit! Her knees threatened to buckle. "Um, no, sir. I'm not."

"Did I say you could talk to me, female?"

Laikyn's eyes narrowed. "I don't believe I asked you if I could, thank you very much."

"Father, this is our mate. Her name is Jennaveve. She healed Lucas from silver poisoning and now, we don't know what is wrong with her." Damien stepped in front of Laikyn.

Kellen growled and pulled her away from the vampire.

"Is she human?" His disdain was clear.

Another rumble shook the foundation.

"What the hell is going on?"

Silence filled the room while she assumed the twins gave their father the run down. Kellen began easing her toward the door to the inner hall.

"So, you brought this wolf to the attention of a vampire. A vampire who has now tried to kill you. And you are just telling me." Eyes as dark as night turned red.

Laikyn was glad she wasn't Damien or Lucas in that moment.

"Mon Chaton, I need you to go to the club and stay with Rowan. I'm going to make sure this fight doesn't come inside this time." His voice brooked no argument.

"Come with me. Let them handle one of their own," she pleaded.

Kellen's growl was her answer. Even in her head she could tell she'd disappointed him. She sent him a feeling of love, which he returned.

"I know you're scared. I promise I'll live long enough to give you a proper punishment."

They reached the doorway while the trio of arguing males were focused on each other. Laikyn leaned up and kissed her mate. *"Stay safe."* Then she left before she made a fool of herself.

"Very smart to send the female away. I will take the Fey to my mate and return."

The male Kellen had yet to be introduced to disappeared, taking Jennaveve with him.

"Is he always like that?" Kellen looked at Damien and a now healed Lucas.

Damien nodded. "Actually, he was quite cordial."

Kellen placed his hands on his hips. "Well, let me explain how this is gonna go down."

"No, let me tell you how this is going to go down." The deep voice had Kellen spinning, his claws out.

He heard two identical male voices yelling at him, but his instincts kicked in, unleashing his inner war beast. Shifting to the Direwolf, something only a few of his kind could, his iron claws ripped from his knuckles as he pushed the vampire king onto the table his son had been lying on.

"Don't ever sneak up on me, motherfucker. You won't come out the winner." Kellen allowed the male to see his own death flash before his eyes. It was good to be alpha.

"Holy fuck. What are you?" Lucas asked.

"He's a true alpha." The male beneath him blinked. "Allow me to get up."

It wasn't a show of submission, but enough for Kellen to back off. "Now, are you going to introduce yourself?" Kellen pushed off, getting to his feet, keeping to the form he'd shifted into.

"My name is Damikan Cordell. Vampire King if you will." He nodded his head.

"Alright. I understand you know more about what we are facing, but these are my people. I don't want them at any more risk than they are. If we can face these pieces of shit outside, then that is what we do. Feel me?"

Damikan shook his head. "I don't want to feel you."

Lucas sighed. "Father, he means—"

The vampire king raised his hand. "They are coming. Let's go. I have help waiting to arrive when the sun is set. They will keep your people safe and fight this battle with us. You may stay inside as well."

Kellen flicked his claws open. The metal clang had the three vampires' eyes widening.

"Well, alright then. If you take the head off, they cannot rise. Rip out their heart, and same thing. Most other wounds will only piss them off," Damien said as they opened the door.

The sun was setting, it's pink and orange glow beautiful in the sky. "Why was the ground shaking if they weren't already here?" Kellen asked. "And how are you here?" Kellen looked at Damikan.

"I am King," Damikan noted.

Between one second and the next the lot was empty, and then several men dropped to the ground. The members of his pack having been instructed to clear it out of their vehicles, leaving the area open for the fight.

"I'm assuming these are your men since you're not attacking?"

"What the hell is that?" A red-haired giant of a male asked.

"That would be a Direwolf alpha you want to be nice to." Damikan looked toward the woods. "The difference between good and evil is easy most times, wolf. You'll smell the difference." He pointed to his nose.

Kellen remembered the acrid stench from earlier. "Well fuck me."

"No thank you."

Blades were drawn from several of the men's backs, and then they were taking fighting stances.

"These are my father's elite guards," Lucas explained.

"Why did he bring them?"

"My mother would allow none other. Believe me, you want only the best, and these are the best. Besides my brother and me, that is."

Beings poured out of the woods, cutting off their communication. They were outnumbered six to one, but Kellen noticed the men with the Cordells didn't back away. His beast rose up to meet the battle as he noticed one trying to slip past the battling vampires. Instant recognition hit him. This was the male who'd taken his mate from her dream state.

Kellen stalked the vampire, effortlessly taking the head off one of the lesser vampires who tried to get in his way. Blood coated him, fueling the beast inside. He ducked a headless body being tossed aside, the smell of rotting flesh no longer affecting him. His only goal lay feet from him, trying to gain entrance into the back of his club. He saw the being's hand turn red from whatever protection had been applied to all the entrances thanks to the vampires.

"Hello, little man," Kellen growled from behind Nigel Watson. And he was a small man. Hell, his mate was taller than the male in front of him. Little man syndrome clearly rode this one.

"I'll show you little man," Nigel lashed out with his arm, trying to punch through Kellen's chest.

Laughing Kellen stepped to the side.

Nigel's eyes narrowed, then he clicked his fingers. Snakes slithered up from the ground. The concrete splitting beneath their feet, allowing the serpents to crawl toward their leader.

"What're you gonna do now? Hiss and spit like a reptile?" Kellen wasn't sure how to kill something covered in snakes, but he wasn't allowing this male anywhere near his people.

When the first snake shot out like a missile, he caught it in one of his fists, and ripped it in two. Nigel used the snakes like a gun, throwing them in rapid fire, too many for Kellen to rip apart before they were sinking their fangs into his flesh.

He roared in anger and agony. Deciding to end the man, he launched himself across the space, taking Nigel by surprise, uncaring that the serpents continued to attack him. Slamming his fist into the chest, sinking his iron claws past skin and bones, intent on one thing. He could hear the pounding of the man's heart. Ignoring the bites sinking into him, his hand latched onto the organ while his other handheld the back of Nigel's head, keeping the male from sinking his teeth into his jugular.

"You can't defeat me," Nigel shouted.

Kellen stared down, pulling his fist back. "The fuck if I can't," he snarled as he jerked the last inch out of the chest cavity, the black blood oozing around the heart, Kellen tossed Nigel away from him.

Damien and Lucas came toward him, the snakes falling off as their master fell to the ground.

"Here, let me dispose of that," Damien offered.

He let the Cordell twin take the thing from him, a feeling of lightheadedness swamped him. His knees buckled, making him hit the ground.

"Well, damn, boy." Damikan came over and squatted in front of him. "This might hurt a little."

Blood clouded his vision. He wasn't sure what the hell the vampire king was talking about. Hell, at that moment he wanted to lie down, only thoughts of reaching out to Laikyn one last time before he faded away kept him from doing so. Yeah, he knew he was dying, and damn if he wasn't pissed. However, he knew he'd done what was right. They'd destroyed the vampires, and his people were safe.

"Goddess, save me from the mumbling of fools," Damikan said.

Kellen raised his middle finger, not realizing he'd been mumbling out loud. "

White hot heat bathed him. Searing pain followed, making him wish for his favorite bottle of hard liquor or two. He tried to raise his fists. Tried to push the men away from him. The absolute lack of power had him fighting the invisible bonds that held him. A growl unlike any he'd ever unleashed shook him to the core, then he was standing. The Cordell twins along with their father stood several feet away along with the contingent of vampires they'd brought with.

"What the hell just happened?" He asked between his teeth, not recognizing his own voice.

Damikan gave a careless shrug. "I healed you. We are even."

He blinked, expecting to feel blood again. "What exactly are we even for?"

"You saved my son. I saved you. We are even."
Damikan stared at him, dark eyes identical to his
sons waited for Kellen.

Kellen held out his hand, then stared at the iron
claws. He forced his body to shift back to human.
"Thank you," Kellen said, glad his voice was back
to normal. He didn't want to face Laikyn looking
like a monster. Only a few of his pack had seen his
other form. He wasn't sure how she'd react if, or
rather when she saw it.

"See, that is how a real leader reacts." Damikan
took Kellen's hand. "I have a feeling we will be
seeing each other again. Until next time, wolf."

In a blink his lot was empty save for Damian
and Lucas. The carnage left behind would take a
miracle to clean and get rid of. He wasn't sure how
they'd explain it to the humans let alone where
they'd dispose of it all.

"Alright, let's get this done," Lucas clapped.

Had Kellen not seen the male near death only
hours before, he'd not believe there was ever
anything wrong with him. With a nod, Kellen went

to get a few of his men, when Damien put his hand on his shoulder.

"We got this," Damien said.

Magic exploded, taking the mess that was their parking lot and returning it to what it was before.

"Damn, do you do windows too?" Kellen joked, looking around.

Lucas laughed. "Nah, we leave that up to the females."

He said goodbye to the Cordells then headed to the entrance, unsure what he'd find inside. He hadn't felt Laikyn in his mind since the battle had begun. His body felt strung as tight as a bow string.

When he opened the door, she threw herself at him, kissing him with a need he met.

"Don't you ever try to shut me out. Ever again," she said between kisses.

He lifted her by the ass, her long legs wrapping around his hips. The members of his pack stood behind her, silently witnessing their leader being chastised by his mate, and he truly gave no fucks.

Later, he'd remind her who was in charge. But, in that moment he wanted to get lost in her taste.

A loud cough had him tugging Laikyn's head away from his mouth. He nipped her lower lip, soothing the little ache. "When I get you home, I'm not letting you out of my sight or bed for twenty-four hours or more."

"Good," she agreed.

"Who's on clean up, boss?" Bodhi asked.

"The Cordells took care of it."

Syn sauntered up to him. "I'm glad you're safe. You know I'd kick your ass if you got hurt, and then I'd have to be all grown up and shit. I'm not ready for all that yet."

"Love you, too." Kellen pulled his sister in for a side hug.

"Do you realize you still have Laikyn in your arms?" Syn asked.

"Yep, not letting her go till I get her home." Kellen kept one firm hand on his mate's ass.

Laikyn tapped him on the shoulder. "How you gonna drive with me like this?"

He let his sister go, then tugged on Laikyn's hair. He truly did enjoy pulling the heavy mass. "I'll manage. Don't you worry your pretty little head."

His mate sighed. Her breathy moan had his cock jerking in his jeans.

He barked orders to the members of his pack who were staying there, knowing Coti and Wyck planned to make sure everything ran smoothly. Xan and Breezy eyed him from the corner along with Rowan and Lyric. He watched his sister leave with two of her girlfriends, wishing Bodhi would get his head out of his ass.

"Rowan, I'll have a couple pack members take your two babies back to you tomorrow. Thanks for letting us use them to get Lucas out."

The big ex-SEAL tilted his head. "No problem. That's what pack does."

"I'm out. You guys hanging around or leaving?"

"Nope, Lyric has decided the practice is over. It's time to start making babies," Rowan rumbled.

Lyric punched her mate in the arm, then jumped into his arms as he led the way out the door, waving at the room at large as she yelled, "I'm going home to make babies."

"How about you, Xan?"

"We're still practicing. Often." Xan winked.

Kellen shook his head. "I swear, you boys are fucked in the head. I know how to make babies. I also know how to keep from making them until my mate and I are ready."

Laikyn licked the shell of his ear. "I'm ready to go home and fuck whenever you are, Sir."

Like a switch to a trigger, his body went from relaxed, to eager in a heartbeat. "We're out."

He left, tossing his hand up in a farewell to the rest of his pack. His mate buried her face in his neck, licking at the mating mark she'd made there.

At his XV, he stopped next to the driver's door, making a quick decision. "Pants. Off."

Green eyes glowed. "What?"

"Now, Laikyn." He reached behind him and unlocked her ankles.

Standing, his mate shimmied out of her pants and undies, standing in her shirt and bra, he nodded. He unfastened his buckle, then the snap and zipper.

Her eyes widened at his rock-hard erection standing at attention. "Climb on, baby."

"Is this safe?"

He gave her his most dominating look, holding out his hand. She bent and tossed her clothing into the passenger seat, then with the eagerness of an aroused female, hopped into his arms. He held her easily, the smell of her sweet cream the best thing he'd ever tasted.

Again, he anchored her to him with one arm on her ass, the other he fisted in her hair. "You ready for the ride of your life?"

"I'm ready for anything and everything with you."

Wetness coated the head of his dick as he eased her onto his cock. Slowly he entered her in increments, while he kissed a path across her jaw, down her neck to the mating mark. As he bit down, he felt her pussy clench easing his entry.

Climbing behind the wheel, with Laikyn on his lap, he hit the control to give them more room. Shutting the door, the blacked-out windows kept the world at bay while he had his mate right where he wanted her. "Show me your nipples. Are they hard?"

She nodded.

"Take your shirt off." He held her hips, guiding her in a slow up and down motion.

Laikyn looked around, but pulled the top off, leaving her in a lacy demi-bra. Without him having to tell her, she reached behind and unsnapped the latch, tossing it onto her pile of clothing.

"Fucking perfect." And she was. Too damn perfect.

He took her right nipple into his mouth, suckling, biting on the hardened tip. Her moan was music to his ears. His fingers bit into her hips, lifting her faster, bringing their bodies together harder. The sound of flesh hitting, combined with their breathing, the only noise in the vehicle.

"Kellen. I'm going to come. Please. Let me come," she pleaded, head thrown back against the steering wheel.

He moved his lips to the left breast, wanting to put his marks all over her body. "Come for me, baby."

She screamed. The muscles of her pussy clamping down on his cock had his eyes crossing, but he kept from coming. When she settled down, he looked into his mate's eyes. "I'll never stop needing to feel you surrounding me. Not my heart, or my body."

"You didn't come." A worried frown on her face.

"No. I will when I get you home. I just needed to feel you. Every second of every day I want you. I have to stop my beast from making you beg for us.

He wants you breathless." Kellen lifted her easily off him.

"Only your wolf?" She asked as he placed her in the passenger seat.

He stopped her before she put her top back on, taking his own off. "Here, you can put this on, but leave yours off. I want my scent surrounding you."

"I love how bossy you are."

He couldn't dispute the fact he was bossy in all things. It was his way. Once she was buckled up, he tucked his dick into his jeans, then started his vehicle. They drove home, their hands entwined.

In his garage, she sat waiting for him to come around. A more perfect female couldn't have been created for him. "Leave your things. I'll get them later." Kellen gathered her into his arms, carrying her through the silent house, into the master suite.

"You know when I was in college all the girls would wish for prince charming or something like that. I would snort and tell them to forget about him. I wanted the wolf. I would get looks, but then after I explained how he could see you better, smell you better, and eat you out so much better, they'd laugh. They had no clue I was speaking with knowledge. Of course, at the time it wasn't experience, but hopefulness."

"Oh, I definitely plan to make you, my meals." He licked his lips. "You're the most delectable thing I've ever had the pleasure of tasting."

"I've craved you. Not just your kisses, but you since I was old enough to know what it meant to be mated was." Laikyn squeezed her arms around his neck.

He placed her on the ground next to his bed. She truly was a work of art. Her pulse beat at the base of her neck. He bent and licked a line from her collarbone up to her ear. "I craved you long before I should have. My desires were so dark, I thought I would scare you away."

She traced his nipple with her nail. "Silly, alpha."

"Are you ready to make love, or get spanked, my mate?"

"How about whatever you decide?" Her incredibly long lashes shielded her eyes from him.

Oh, he really did love how his mate's mind worked. He ripped his shirt from her body, loving the fact she had nothing on beneath. A tremor moved through him at the sight of his marks on her neck and breasts from earlier. They'd be gone by morning, but he loved seeing them.

He lowered his head, licking and sucking one nipple, then the other, savoring her like the sweet treat she was. Laikyn arched, writhing against him, her scent telling him she craved his mouth elsewhere. The bond opened, and he could feel, hear, and see exactly what she wanted and needed. Who was he to deny them both what they wanted and needed?

Chapter Sixteen

Laikyn's entire body was desperate for release even though she'd already came once in the rig. Her skin was too tight, overly sensitized, yet she didn't want to make him rush. She knew if she did, he'd make her wait just to punish her. Of course, Kellen's brand of punishment would be a pleasure in itself. A shudder wracked her as he moved her onto the big bed.

"Kellen," she moaned on a breathless whisper.

His hands brushed her arms above her head, but he didn't tie her to the posts this time. The rough pads of his fingertips had goose bumps raising on her flesh up and down her entire body. Then he was kneeling over her. Moisture gleamed on the head of his dick making her mouth water for a taste of him. She wanted to drink him in.

His gaze stared down at her, and she knew what he saw. What he wanted. Her complete surrender. Her face flushed; her body ached. The tips of her nipples rose up begging for his attention. Her pussy open for him to fill.

"I'm yours. Whatever, whenever, however you want me."

Her words released him from an invisible tether. He grabbed her knees, and spread her thighs, making a place for his big body.

His breath hissed out of him and then he leaned down, face next to hers. "You are mine. Always have been, always will be."

"Yes, yes." There were no other words to say. She was and would always be his.

At first, she thought he'd stare at her forever, then he merely nodded, then began kissing away her tears. Laikyn hadn't realized she'd shed any. The male stripped her bare, laying her soul wide open, defenseless. Yet she never felt more protected as she was with him.

"You will always be safe with me," he murmured between kisses. When his mouth finally poised over her mound, she raised up to look at his dark head. Glowing blue eyes stared at her as his tongue flicked out, sweet torment had her shivering.

Kellen hummed against her flesh, lapping at her taste. One hand lay flat on her belly, the other held her open for him. Laikyn tried to hold still, her hands fisting in the red sheets beneath her.

He brought her close to the brink of coming. Every thrust of his tongue had her writhing, begging for more.

"Please. Need you in me." His tongue darted in and out of her like she wanted his cock to do. She screamed, begged for more, but the diabolical male kept her on edge while he brought her back down without letting her go over. Light teasing strokes all around her, but not where she needed, had her panting. Sweat beading on her body. He had her entire being strung tight, damn near ready to claw the sheets apart.

"You are not quite ready, Mon Chaton." Kellen pushed one broad finger into her.

She whimpered. "I truly am."

He tapped the hood of her clit with the tips of his fingers, the act making her cry out. Laikyn reached down with her right hand; her fingers twitched to touch his soft hair. "May I touch you?"

A wash of arousal flooded her at his nod of approval. "Good girl." His features softened.

Kellen made a show of licking her from clit to bottom, then his hand removed hers from him.

"On your knees, baby." Before she could move herself, he was flipping her over, maneuvering her body how he wanted her. His hand fisted in her hair, turning her head toward him. "I love your luscious ass."

Laikyn licked her lips, wondering if he was going to take her in all ways, but his head shook. "Not yet."

The scent of her arousal rose. He reached between her legs and guided the head of his cock to her entrance and pushed his way in. Then he was surging over her, arms braced next to her. Their heads next to each other. He locked eyes with his mate. "I love you."

Her eyes flared with erotic promise. "Love you more. Forever."

Kellen fucked his mate. No sweet and slow loving. It was raw and hard. He fed her his length, keeping their gazes locked, stretching her. She fit him perfectly, and he found himself racing for release. He had to pause, making sure his mate was with him. "Open yourself to me."

Instantly their mate link opened, and he could feel she was right there, teetering on the edge. The slick wet heat of her pussy kissed his cock as he thrust in and out.

Groaning at pleasure he was sure would kill him, she moved with him, back and forth, squeezing and releasing along his cock. She was wild beneath him, clawing at the sheets as if she was only waiting for him to allow her to let go. "Come for me. Milk my cock. Let me fill you with my seed."

"Fuck, yes. Kellen, I'm coming." Her shout came as her muscles clamped down on his throttling cock. All he could do was hold on, slamming in and out, racing toward his own, and then his canines punched out of his gums. His wolf wanting to claim her as well.

When he sunk his teeth in, her second orgasm hit, taking Kellen with her, roaring loud enough the animals near and far were sure to hear, muscles bunching while he continued to ride out his orgasm.

Finally, when he was spent, he released her neck, then grabbed her by the hair, and turned her to face him, meshing their lips together. Teeth clicked together in the savage kiss. She stripped his soul, then remade him into a better man. He'd seen in her mind the love and devotion she had for him.

Once his dick softened enough, he could slide out, Kellen went to the bathroom for a warm washcloth, wanting to ease his mate. The lovely blush that covered her face and neck thrilled him.

"I love that you can still turn this beautiful pink," he ran his knuckles over her jaw, "even after I have you stripped anywhere, with my cock in your sweet pussy without blinking. Yet, when I clean you up, you blush." He tossed the cloth into the hamper by the door.

He climbed back into bed, pulling her to his side.

"Well, when you put it that way it seems silly." She rolled into him.

"You saw me," he said in the still of the night.

She didn't pretend to misunderstand him, and he loved her even more for it. He knew when they'd connected, he couldn't hide from her. The Direwolf was a part of him he'd only let out a few times. When he'd been chosen as alpha, the goddess had come to him, gifting the special ability to him. He'd not had to unleash the iron claws, or the beast that he'd done tonight since he'd been a young man, and too stupid to control the shift. Xan and Bodhi had been there along with his father. That was the night he'd taken over as the alpha.

"Was your dad scared of you?" He kissed the top of her head at her question.

Kellen was relieved she was more worried for him because his mate was magnificent. He rolled her over. "How did I get so lucky?"

With a gentle roll of his hips, he entered his heaven. The one place he truly belonged without question. One day they'd make a baby, but until then they'd do what his brothers called practicing. His hips rose and fell in a slow rhythm. The frenzy from earlier gone.

His arms wrapped around her, holding her to him while his body rode her in a rocking rhythm that was as old as time. Her body met each thrust of his with hers.

Their souls connecting the same as their bodies. In perfect accord they became one. And one day they'd create a little one who'd be a little of each of them. The thought didn't terrify him. In fact, it made him harder.

"Your eyes are glowing." She traced his brows.

He dropped his head into the crook of her neck, feeling a sense of wonder. "I fucking love you like none other."

Kellen had to shake himself to look back at his mate.

"I feel the same. Come inside me. Let me feel you. I love the way you lock inside me and the warmth of your seed—" he cut her words off with his mouth on hers.

His ass flexed, erection stroking in and out in two, three strokes, and then he was coming, his orgasm taking them both over the edge. Her incredible body accepting all he had to give and taking it with obvious enjoyment.

They both lay panting. He continued to feel his dick twitch and her pussy flex as he spurted come deep inside Laikyn. If she'd been fertile, he would have planted a child in her this night. When he was sure he had nothing left to give, he stilled, but held his weight on his elbows, not wanting to crush her smaller frame.

"Well, I would say we definitely know how to make babies." Laikyn laughed up at him.

Kellen lifted up a little further. "Do you want one soon? A little one?"

She shook her head. "Not yet. I mean I want a little dark-haired boy who looks just like you, but I'd like to wait a little while."

He met her eyes and seeing the honesty there he nodded. "We'll make that decision together."

"Thank you." Tears sparked in the green depths, reminding him of emeralds.

"Why are you crying?"

She sniffed. "I'm just so happy."

He smiled. "Well, you still have yet to be punished, but those will come tomorrow. I'm tired tonight. It takes a lot out of you to kick vampire ass. By the way, I hope you don't like cabbage." He shuddered.

Laikyn laughed while he rolled onto his back. With his mate wrapped in his arms, Kellen didn't think anything could be any more perfect except he and his mate's little ones. He'd make sure they had a son first to protect his little sister. Of course, his daughter would look just like her mother, and would be perfect. The thought had him thinking they'd need to have a couple boys first.

"I don't think it works that way." Laikyn's sleepy voice breathed across his bare chest.

"My children will listen to me even before they are born."

She patted his chest, then fell into sleep. Long minutes later, he looked out the window, staring out at the moon. Surely the goddess wouldn't send him a daughter first. A cloud covered the moon, and he was sure a gentle hand brushed his cheek. Assured all was right in his world, he allowed himself to fall asleep.

The End

Want to read the next book in the Iron Wolves Series? Be sure and pick up Slater's Enchanting Mate?

Want to read how it all began? Check out Lyric's Accidental Mate
Iron Wolves MC book 1

The Iron Wolves Next Generation is Here!

Check out Bad Wolf, Book 1

If you enjoyed this book, you may also enjoy...

The Mystic Wolves Series

The Magic and Mayhem Series

The Ravens of War Series

The Complete Iron Wolves Series Here

Signup For My Newsletter For Accidentally Wolf, Book 1 of the Mystic Wolves

Author's Note

I'm often asked by wonderful readers how they could help get the word out about the book they enjoyed. There are many ways to help out your favorite author, but one of the best is by leaving an honest review. Another great way is spread the word by recommending the books you love, because stories are meant to be shared. Thank you so very much for reading this book and supporting all authors. If you'd like to find out more about Elle's books, visit her website, or follow her on FaceBook, Twitter, Instagram, and other social media sites.

Thank You

Thank you for reading Kellen's Tempting Mate! I hope you loved it!

Did you enjoy meeting Kellen and Laikyn? I really enjoyed getting the alpha to finally admit his feelings. Up next is Slater who you might have met in my SmokeJumpers and LeeLee who y'all will hopefully love. P.S. The Fey Queen who is the alpha's bestie will be in most all the books "wink".

You can also join my Facebook group, Elle Boon's Bombshells, to discuss all things Elle Boon books and see what's going on or coming up in my book world.

Want to stay up to date on upcoming releases in all my series? Be sure to join my VIP newsletter here. I promise your inbox will be filled with the hottest dominating Alphas and exclusive content.

XOXO,

ELLE BOON

About Elle Boon

Elle Boon is a reader first and foremost...and of course if you know her, she's the crazy lady with purple hair. She's also a USA Today Bestselling Author who lives in Middle-Merica as she likes to say... with her husband and Kally Kay, her black lab who also thinks she's her writing partner. (She happens to sit next to her begging for treats and so takes a lot of credit). She has two amazing kids, Jazz and Goob, and is a MiMi to one adorable little nugget named Romy or RomyGirl (greatest job EVER) who has totally won over everyone who sees hers (If anyone says a hair bow is too big, they're crazy). She's known for saying "Bless Your Heart" and dropping lots of F-bombs (I mean lots of F-BOMBS, but who is keeping track?).

She loves where this new journey has taken her and has no plans on stopping. She writes what she loves to read, and that's romance, whether it's about

Navy SEALs, HOT as F**K MC heroes, or paranormal alphas. #dontlookdown is a thing you will need to google. "Wink" With all her stories, you're guaranteed a happily ever after, no matter what twisted thing her mind has come up with. Her biggest hope is that after readers have read one of her stories, they fall in love with her characters as much as she has. She loves creating new worlds and has more just waiting to be written. Elle believes in happily ever after and can guarantee you will always get one within the pages of her books.

Connect with Elle online. She loves to hear from you:

www.elleboon.com

https://www.facebook.com/elle.boon

https://www.facebook.com/Elle-Boon-Author-1429718517289545/

https://twitter.com/ElleBoon1

https://www.facebook.com/groups/RacyReads/

https://www.facebook.com/groups/1405756769719931/

https://www.goodreads.com/author/show/812008

5.Elle_Boon

https://www.bookbub.com/authors/elle-boon

https://www.instagram.com/elleboon/

http://www.elleboon.com/newsletter

Other Books by Elle Boon

Ravens of War

Selena's Men

Two For Tamara

Jaklyn's Saviors

Kira's Warriors

Akra's Demons

Mystic Wolves

Accidentally Wolf

His Perfect Wolf

Jett's Wild Wolf

Bronx's Wounded Wolf

A Fey's Wolf

Their Wicked Wolf

Atlas's Forbidden Wolf

SmokeJumpers

FireStarter

Berserker's Rage

A SmokeJumpers Christmas

Choosing His Mate, A Prequel to FireStarter

Coming Soon

■■

Iron Wolves MC

Lyric's Accidental Mate

Xan's Feisty Mate

Kellen's Tempting Mate

Slater's Enchanted Mate

Dark Lovers

Bodhi's Synful Mate

Turo's Fated Mate

Dark Embrace, The Fey Queen's Story

Arynn's Chosen Mate

Coti's Unclaimed Mate

■■

Miami Nights

Miami Inferno

Rescuing Miami

■■

Standalone

Wild and Dirty, Wild Irish Series

Big Deal Sweetheart, Sweetheart Colorado

■■

SEAL Team Phantom Series

Delta Salvation

Delta Recon

Delta Rogue

Delta Redemption

Mission Saving Shayna

Protecting Teagan

∎∎

The Royal Sons MC Series

Royally Twisted

Royally Taken

Royally Tempted

Royally Treasured

Royally Broken

Royally Saved

Royally Chosen Christmas

Royally Beloved

Royally Targeted

Royally Ruthless, In the Royal Harlot's Anthology

Royally Inked

∎∎

Royally Judged, Coming Soon

Magic and Mayhem

The Lion's Witchy Mate

The Leopards Witchy Mate

The Wannabe Witchy Mate, Coming Soon

Standalone

Shaw's Wild Mate, Coming Soon

A Cursed Hallows Eve Anthology

Their Dragon Mate

Her Dragon Mate, Coming Soon

The Dragon's Mate, Once You Shifter Anthology

IRON WOLVES - THE NEXT GENERATION

Bad Wolf *– Xian & Egypt, Book 1*

Tempted Wolf *– Jagger & Willow, Book 2*

The Vampire's Wolf *– Liv & Kahn, Book 3*

Embrace A Wolf *– Jaxon & Piper, Book*